The Redwoods

By Kayando Wolf

Chapter One

The Wintuks had everything. They were the perfect family. The perfect little Wintuks, all perfectly tucked away in the outskirts of Oyster Shoals, somewhere in northern California. Jerry was a stay at home dad, while his wife, Jovie, was an established author. They had three children, Sanjay, Sierra, and Sherpa. The smell of fresh redwood and sap filled the air inside their newly built home, surrounded by of course—redwoods. Not only was the house surrounded by redwoods, but constructed from them too. One would think that's a horrible idea, due to the high costs of redwood. To Jovie however, this was the best long-term idea, considering redwood was poisonous to termites.

Termites be gone! I've outsmarted you this time, you fuckers, Jovie would think to herself as a constant pat on the back.

"Good thinking, Jove," Jerry would say to her, as a constant reassurance, complimenting her ideas with encouragement. He was always such a supportive husband.

"This place is finally coming altogether, don't you think?" asked Jerry.

"Oh yea, this couldn't be better," Jovie responded. She couldn't help but notice a smirk smear across his face. They both stared at one another, waiting for a queue.

"I'm sorry hun, your midwest twang will never get old to me but don't get me wrong, you know I love it, and I love you," he said while chuckling. Pulling her close to his chest now, giving her a peck on the top of her head.

Sanjay ran in, joining in on the roasting of mom that was taking place, "Oh, don't ya know!" he yelled, attempting his best midwest accent. It was poor, but Jovie giggled with her son, trying not to bruise his ego. She remembered how delicate egos were at the age of thirteen.

They had adopted Sanjay from India when he was only six months old, he was their first child. It wasn't until years later that they gave birth to Sierra and Sherpa through In-vitro fertilization, or as some would say test-tube babies; once they realized they had complications getting pregnant. The laughter of Sierra and Sherpa could be heard through the hallways, getting louder and louder, until they reached the living room. The girls noticed the three of them hugging and sprinted over, afraid of missing out on attention from mom and dad, or even their big brother. Sherpa, the youngest of the three, ran over and face-planted so hard into mom's ass, she appeared to have bounced off, ricocheting back onto the wood floor. The whole family stopped now, staring at one another, not sure if they should laugh or run over to Sherpa's aid. Everyone waited patiently for a sign.

"Dat was funny!" she delightfully shrieked. They all started smiling now at one another in relief.

"Sherpa, where are your glasses?" Jerry asked.

"Dey fell off daddy, over der somewhere," she said while pointing back towards the hallway.

"I'll get 'em!" Sierra exclaimed willingly, running off with a blanket wrapped around her neck like a cape. "Middle child to the rescuuue!" echoed as she ran to start her mission. Sierra could see her little sister's glasses poking out from the half-open door leading down to the basement.

"Ah-hah! There you are," she said to herself.

As she bent over to pick them up, they quickly got pulled back in.

Clink, clank, clunk…

She peered down through the door, observing the glasses through the slits between the stairs. Being the good big sister that Sierra was, she began to make her way down the freshly constructed stairs. She loved the smell of redwood and sap, taking in big whiffs as she walked. Suddenly, the smell of fresh redwood diminished. It now reeked of rotten eggs. She quickly grabbed the glasses and ran back upstairs, slamming the door shut.

"Hey! No slamming doors!" she could hear her mom yell.

"It reeks down there!" Sierra replied.

"Yea reeks of fresh redwood," Jovie said pleasantly.

"No mom, I like that smell. It smelled like rotten eggs down there".

Her dad walked over, "You sure you didn't just let one slip, Sierra? Hm?"

"Yea, do you need to check yer pants, Sara?" little Sherpa questioned.

"It's SI-ER-RA, how many times do I have to tell you? At least I'm not named after a mattress company," Sierra teased.

"Sierra!" her parents yelled scoldingly.

"I'm named affer a mad dress copy?" Sherpa pronounced as best she could.

Sanjay intervened, "Technically, Sierra is also a mattress company," he said proudly.

Both Jerry and Jovie shot each other a look that said, *how the hell did he even know that?*

"How did you even know that Sanjay?" Jovie questioned her son.

"I was at Ron's house and after his parents asked my sisters' names, they both giggled and I heard Ron's dad whisper to his mom, 'maybe they name them after the mattress they, you know,' and I had to think about it for a few minutes, but then it hit me—SEX!" Jerry and Jovie were trying to both stay serious at this point, but it proved to be more difficult then they had thought.

"Ok, first off, just so we're clear, that's not the case" Jovie said calmly while trying to not crack a smile, though you could hear it slipping out through her midwest accent.

Sierra stomped out of the house in frustration, upset that no one investigated the eggy smell she had just endured.

"I'm going for a waaaalk!" she yelled out.

"No further than the creek, rememberrr!" her dad yelled back.

"I knooow!"

It was obvious they were shooting sass back and forth to one another through their tones. Sierra eventually made her way down the path from the house that would lead her to the creek. It was springtime, her favorite time of year. The pathway's perimeter was surrounded by wildflowers of lupine and poppies, with vines of prickly cucumber tangling about. The hanging prickly cucumbers always reminded her of Christmas ornaments, dangling from the tree branches. There was one redwood tree larger than the rest, it was super-colossal compared to the other towering trees. The massive trunk had a triangular opening, an entrance to the inside. Overgrown fern covered the entrance, making it hidden from the rest of the world. Inside was Sierra and Sanjay's world, their fort, their safe spot. They had discovered it a while back while the house was still being built, taking extra tile flooring and laying it inside. Even taking the front door mat and placing it inside—which Jovie still believed just got lost during the move. It was one of those customized mats, displaying, ***The Wintuks***, printed on it.

Sierra cut off the path, moving the fern out of her way to crawl into the redwood trunk. Inside they had a battery-powered lantern that she turned on and two small boxes, one filled with snacks and the other with a mixture of random stuff. They had labeled the outside of the boxes, 'SnACkS' and 'StUFF.' The latter box had some pens and pencils, notebooks, a Rubik cube, a few R.L. Stine books, a walk talkie, and a pocket knife. Sierra plucked the Rubik cube out from the box and began analyzing it, twisting and turning the toy.

Sniff, sniff.

What's that? she thought as she sniffed in again.

"Are you kidding me," she mumbled under her breath. It smelled of rotten eggs—again. She crawled out of the fort, brushing her knees off and continued walking towards the nearby creek. Sierra stood at the edge of the creek, listening to the calmness of the water flowing over the hundreds of pebbles that laid at the bottom. Croaking noises surrounded her as toads swam and hopped around.

Crooooooak.

That smell is getting stronger, she thought.

Crooooooak.

It was becoming harder and harder to enjoy the ambiance with that stomach-wrenching smell. She looked up to see a shirtless man on the other side of the creek. He was wearing some sort of animal head over his, with large horns coming out from it. Sierra could feel her eyes watering with fear as she stared through the trees at this…thing? *This man-thing?* It's still, unblinking eyes were staring into her lively ones. He began waving at her. She started breathing harder and heavier now, scared of the unknown and what was unfolding in front of her eyes. There was a rustling of leaves, her eyes darted towards the sound and there stood another…thing. A shirtless female this time with a horned animal's head over her own also. Slowly, more and more of these people—or things appeared from behind the trees. She wasn't sure what the hell they were, but by God, they looked as if they were from Hell if her pure mind had to take a gander. The creek that ran clear before was now flowing with thick sticky blood and all the toads were floating belly up. The horrid rotten egg smell was so strong, you would think if you lit a match, a forest fire would erupt. Sierra's scrawny chicken legs felt weak, numb from the fear that was spreading like a planted seed in her mind. The seed felt like it was bursting open now, sprouting and growing roots out to every limb and joint in her body. Suffocating her nerves with fear, making her eventually collapse to the forest floor.

The cool spring breeze caressed Sierra's skin, giving her goosebumps, making her come to. She could feel her eyes slowly opening, seeing slits of light shine down through the tree branches above. She continued to lay there as this mesmerizing sight provided comfort. The smell of the forest and sweet flowers filled her tiny nose now.

Carefully, she began sitting up—*What's this?*

A bouquet of white flowers fell from her chest. She groggily rubbed her eyes, *yep, still there,* she confirmed.

"Go ahead, eat them," a voice urged her from behind. She turned around to see something kneeling to her level, squatting with hands clasped, resting on the top of their thighs. It appeared devilish, with horns and skin that reminded her of the obsidian arrowheads she and her family would find camping sometimes. It had the most enormous hands or claws, or whatever they were—she'd ever seen in her life. With long sharp black nails that were perfectly sharpened to a point at the ends. The smell of eggs came back too soon. It was much more potently powerful this time, making her gag.

The voice began laughing now, "Oh, Sierra, I don't smell that bad do I?" A sharp-toothed smile spread across *his* face as *his* lips curled back, exposing some drool in the corner. *He* began grunting and growling now as *he* focused in on her fear. *His* vocals were deep and out of this world, Sierra could almost feel it move throughout her body, just like those damn roots of fear spreading to her limbs. Too much drool had collected in the corner of *his* smile now. Sierra stood frozen, as she stared at the drool creeping down *his* face, then to *his* chin. It hung there like an icicle, until too heavy for surface tension, falling to its demise. Gravity was doing an excellent job right now at pulling that drool right out of *his* upwards grin. *His* eyes were completely callous, the entire pupil and iris were solid black, while what should have been the whites of the eye, appeared to be full of blood.

"I said eat them! Fucking eat them, Sierra!" *he* growled at her, spit flying from his mouth onto her face. Poor Sierra was shaking now, feeling like a statue about to crack at any moment due to physical stress. She could feel her face was hot and wet from all the tears that had been streaming down, while snot had collected atop her upper lip. At this moment, gravity was not working in her benefit.

"Eat them, Sierra," *he* urged again, threatening her with *his* dagger-like nail under her chin, resting it against her throat. "You don't want to end belly up like those toads, do you?" *he* threatened. She picked up the white flowers now, eating them while shaking uncontrollably. All she could taste was a mixture of what she could only imagine nature itself would taste like and salt from her snot.

"Good girl, now run off, get out of here!" *he* demanded. She darted in the opposite direction, making her way back into the fort. Moving the fern out of the way, she scurried into the tree trunk like a mouse into a hole in the wall. She clicked the lantern off and sat there with her hands covering her mouth as she breathed heavily in and out. She could see glimpses of *him* through the fern as *he* paced around, then, as if he knew she was staring at him, *he* turned towards her direction and stopped.

Kneeling in the distance, *he* continued to stare at her through the brush as she bit her shirt sleeve to keep from screaming.

Static ... ... static.

"Turn the light on, Sierra," *he* urged through the walkie talkie. She stayed still, clenching onto her shirt sleeve harder now. "Sierra, I said turn the light on," *he* instructed again. She reached over to turn the dial on, while her hand shook uncontrollably.

Click.

She screamed in horror as she looked around to see the inside of the fort appeared to be bleeding now. Bleeding blood instead of sap, it dripped down the insides of the trunk.

"Run!" *he* yelled, laughing as she crawled out. She was tripping and falling as she tried her best to make her legs function normally again.

She ran not only like a chicken with its head cut off, but cut off and thrown in front of her like a dangling carrot. She ran through that forest like getting her detached chicken head back depended on it. Running as fast as she could through the woods was making her legs feel like they were burning from the inside out.

Thump!

––––––––––

"Oh my God, sweetheart! What happened? Tell us what happened, baby," Sierra could hear her mom ask.

"Where am I?" Sierra quietly questioned.

"In the hospital, hunny" her dad answered. Sierra looked up and could see her baby sister was crying and big brother looked worried.

What am I supposed to tell them? she thought. Her family would think she was insane if she told them what happened back in the redwoods. How badly she wished all of this was just a horrible nightmare.

"What are yer doing, Sara?" little Sherpa asked.

"SI-ER-RA, not Sara, and I'm pinching myself to make sure I'm not dreaming," she answered.

"Are you dweaming?" Sherpa inquired.

"Unfortunately, no" Sierra responded. She could see her baby sister pinching herself now, investigating this new technique.

"I'm not dweaming eider," she said confidently after her pinching experiment.

The doctor walked in with that sternly doctor-look that most of them seem to display. He lowered his glasses now, tilting his head down so his eyes peered over the rim. He reminded Sierra of the way her mother would look at her when she was disappointed. Not mad of course, just disappointed.

"Do you know why you're here, Sierra?" he asked. She shook her head indicating she did not. "Well, your family went to look for you after you didn't come home and found you lying in the woods by your house. You had run straight into a tree and it knocked you out. You've got a pretty decent sized bump on your forehead, a concussion even. You also were found holding some white flowers, along with some vomit on your clothes. Sound familiar? You know those are extremely toxic flowers, called lily of the valley. We found trace amounts of it in your system, indicating you ingested it. This plant causes disorientation, blurry vision, and vomiting just to name a few. I'm assuming you ate the flower and at some point felt some of the symptoms, leading up to you running into a tree".

Jovie could feel a lump of emotions had developed in her throat. She was trying so hard to keep it together but the ball of emotions that was throbbing in her throat was so painful now, that she had to choke it out. Letting it escape from her throat, she cried and held Sierra now, kissing her forehead where a thick square piece of gauze was taped on. This act of maternal instinct finally resulted in Sierra sobbing now too. The smell of her mom was so emotionally reactive, like two elements coming together to form as one.

"Hunny, where did those flowers come from? Your eleven years old, I know you know better than to eat something like that. You don't even know what it is or what it will or could do to you" Jerry asked. He almost felt guilty for what had happened. Deep down he knew this wasn't his fault, but at the same time, he felt somewhat partly responsible since he primarily took care of the kids while Jovie worked all day; not to mention some nights. Slumped over her computer, typing away behind a closed door, creating another best-seller. She was the breadwinner, that was for sure.

"I know dad, you're right, I do know better than to do that" she responded softly. In his mind, Jerry let out a sigh of relief. He felt a little bit better hearing his daughter's validation out loud, especially for all-around to hear.

Jovie could sense this, she leaned over and whispered into Jerry's ear, "I love you. You're an amazing dad, I hope you know that." Again, validation at it's finest. He began feeling a little bit less on edge. His guiltiness was fading away, while his heart rate was slowing down now to a more steady pace.

"I picked them," Sierra answered.

"Where?" Sanjay asked.

"I forget," she replied as calmly as possible. He knew she was full of it.

Why is she lying? he thought.

He knows I'm lying, Sierra thought as she stared blankly back at Sanjay. She stared into his dark eyes, imagining them as magic eight balls, like the one they always played with at home.

If his eyes could predict a fortune right now, it would say, 'You're full of shit and I know it.' Maybe if I shook him hard enough I would get lucky and it would change to, 'Try again later,' she imagined. That was wishful thinking.

The Wintuks agreed she needed her rest and to drop the curious case of—what the fuck happened to Sierra, until a later time at home.

Chapter Two

Three weeks passed by since the Wintuks arrived back home from the hospital. Sierra has been depressed and rarely leaves her bedroom. She only has been coming out of her cave of a bedroom to eat, yet it seems she plays with her food more so than eats it.

Jerry and Jovie sat on the front porch, sharing a bottle of wine on the bench they found to be their favorite. Always sitting in the same places on the bench, just like they did so every night in their bed. This was their special evening treat, their special moment together—their creature of habit they tended to. The air was warm enough to not wear a jacket, yet cool enough it felt slightly crisp outside. Not too much of the sun was left, just the remnants of it were shining through the redwoods, highlighting particles floating throughout the forest. The sunset had a reddish glow this evening, covering the tree's bark with a ruby tone while making the spears of light piercing through the trees appear a blood orange color.

"Beautiful, isn't it?" she implied.

"Truly spectacular," he agreed as they clinked wine glasses.

"Looks like a Bob Ross painting that we just poured a bottle of red wine over," she pointed out.

"You should use that in one of your books," he responded. They both smiled at each other regarding this corny idea.

"I still don't get it, why won't Sierra talk to us?" Jovie asked.

"She'll come around, but it's bothering me a lot too," Jerry said.

"I mean, we both damn well know she didn't pick those flowers, they don't even grow around here. Someone gave them to her, and that scares the shit out of me," she confessed while staring at her husband. Both of them stared at one another, trying to look for answers in each other's eyes.

Nothing.

"Mama! Papa!"—both of them jumped up and ran into the house, following Sherpa's voice upstairs. By the time they reached her room, Sanjay and Sierra had already made an entrance. Sherpa's cute little chubby finger was pointed out the bedroom window. Their eyes followed her gaze. Nothing was there, just the tall grass swaying back and forth, red reflections from what was left of the sun bouncing off the polished leaves.

"I don't see anything, Sherpa. Geez, did you fart? It freakin' reeks in here," Sanjay said while waving his hand in front of his face.

"Sanjay, don't use that word," Jovie instructed.

"What word?" he asked.

"Freakin'," she responded while cringing.

Then, something large rose above the tall swaying grass that previously appeared peaceful. It was *him,* the demon-looking being from the woods. *He* was just standing there..staring. Sierra could feel her eyes well up, her vision becoming blurry within seconds from an overdose of tears.

Her parents both stared over at her, asking, "Sierra?"

All she could do was swallow the emotional bullet back down her throat, she wasn't ready to shoot her mouth yet.

The next thing Jerry knew, he was charging out the back door that led to that part of the property—where that horned thing was. He was armed with his Remington shotgun and ready to come face to face with whatever this person or thing was that was traumatizing and harassing his family. He saw the look in Sierra's eyes, the fear that was dominating her soul. He knew this man—or thing was part of it. Jerry missed his baby girl, he missed his happy-go-lucky baby. He was ready to do whatever it took to fuck this asshole up and protect his family.

Aw shit, Jovie thought to herself. She went with her instincts and ran to the master bedroom to grab the other rifle they had, pulling it down from the top shelf in the closet, unlocking the combination lock without hesitation. She informed the kids to go to Sanjay's room, lock the door, and call the police.

"Alright Jovie, focus now…focuuus," she said aloud to herself while aiming the rifle out of the bedroom window. *What the hell is this thing? It can't be human, maybe half?* She kept debating back and forth in her head. "Damnit Jovie, pay attention" she lectured herself.

She focused as her husband played superman. *Goddammit, why did he have to go out there?* she thought as she could see something else moving from the corner of her eye.

"Sanjaaaay! Get back inside! What the hell are you doing!" Jovie screamed out. *Oh great, just what we need right now, superman and superman in training role play. For fuck's sake,* she thought.

Bang! Bang!

Jovie had shot the thing. Both Jerry and Sanjay stared up at her in the window, surprised but relieved at the same time. By this time they could hear the sirens of the police cars pulling onto the property.

Jovie hurried down the stairs to meet up with the group of them all conversing.

"How did you guys get here so fast? Its at least a forty-five minute drive up this mountain?" Jerry asked the cops.

"We were scopin' out our next hunting place. You hunt, Jerry?" the cop responded.

"Over here! I shot the bastard, he's over here in the grass. You can see where it's flattened down from his body" she said while pointing.

"He? Well, ma'am, is this a person or an animal? How did you make that determination?" one of the officers questioned.

"We don't know sir, it looked insane, it— it—," and before Sanjay could finish, they had arrived at the death scene.

"Um, it's a deer, folks," the officer pointed out calmly. "Oh, I see ma'am, you implied he, because of the antlers. Damn! Look at those things! You got yourself quite a buck here, lady! Buck be a ladyyy, tonight!" the officer melodically said in his best Frank Sinatra impression. He was obviously proud of himself for making that corny reference, while no one around him laughed, instead cringed. "Tough crowd," the officer mumbled.

"Do you have kids?" Sanjay asked the officer.

"What? No, why?" the officer responded.

"Because, my dad doesn't even make 'dad jokes' as bad as that one," Sanjay nonchalantly said.

Both Jovie and Jerry responded at the same time with, "Sanjaaaay." Sanjay knew when his parents said his name in that tone, it essentially meant they agreed with him, but not with him announcing it to the world.

The officer still had a confused look on his face, Sanjay mumbled, "Sorry, officer."

Eventually, the officers left, believing the family had mistaken a deer for a creep.

I mean, what else were they going to think? Jerry thought. *Maybe it was just a deer after all? That would make the most logical and reasonably realistic sense. Either that or some fuck face was dressing up and terrorizing his family.* Jerry knew he should get rid of that dead deer, but it was pitch black outside now.

"I'll take care of it tomorrow morning," he said to his wife.

She didn't seem too concerned about this and instead asked, "Jer, what was that thing? We're not crazy, right? I mean..we all saw it." Jerry could feel his insides turning at the thought of this, slowly but surely turning as if his intestines were clothes inside of a washing machine, and that washing machine was his stomach. "It didn't even look human, Jer," she continued. Now he could feel his twisting stomach intensify, turning quicker and stronger, it was on the last spin cycle. The part of the cycle that spins so hard that the machine starts bouncing around, making a ruckus, because you thought to only put shoes in there was a bright idea.

Blah!

He had vomited.

"Oh, hunny!" Jovie cried out, "let's clean you up."

Sherpa was in her bedroom, Jerry and Jovie had just tucked her in. She laid there, holding her stuffed monkey, Boo, and was admiring the glow in the dark plastic stars on her ceiling. She was so proud of those stars, especially the planets. She smiled at the thought of the day her daddy held her up high enough so that she could reach the ceiling to place the planet ones on herself. She loved the feeling of contributing and helping like most children did. The thought of this made her smile and kiss her monkey on the forehead. The rustling of grass could be heard from outside her bedroom window.

Rustle…rustle…

Sherpa tip-toed her tiny feet as quietly as possible to the window as she and Boo tactfully peered over.

He was out there, feasting on the deer. Sherpa stared all glassy and wide-eyed, both disturbed and mesmerized by what she was witnessing. She continued to watch as *he* grabbed ahold of the buck's antlers, pulling so quick and hard, successfully detaching the head. Then raising the deer's head to *his* mouth, gnawing on it like it was a fat turkey leg. Blood was dripping out from its detached neck, then, almost as if its scent attracted more predators, Sherpa could see movement coming from the redwoods. Six figures appeared, three males and three females. They looked just like what Sierra had seen previously in the woods. Shirtless, accompanied by an animals's head over theirs..some were horned, while others had antlers. Little Sherpa and Boo watched in fear as they moved in closer to the deceased, like vultures do with a dying animal. Then, she could see them land on all fours and began running towards the food source. They reminded her of the tigers from the zoo when the caretaker would throw a piece of meat in the exhibit. She covered Boo's eyes, whispering to the stuffed monkey, "Don't look!" She was too scared to continue watching, running back to her bed, and hiding under the covers.

Little Sherpa found it harder and harder to breathe under the covers since all she could smell now was rotten eggs, coughing here and there to readjust her throat. She became so fed up with the smell that she peeled the covers off, caught off guard by what was on her bed.

For a split second, Sanjay awoke in bed thinking he had to get up for school soon. During this sleepy haze, he realized he was still on spring break, dropping his head back down on his pillow, smiling at this delightful discovery.

Fuck yeah, he thought to himself. That was something he would never say aloud, only in his mind, *so why the fuck not,* he thought. Plus, as a thirteen-year-old, cursing was something new to him. It was adult-like! It meant you were cool, or whatever you were saying was important, or in some cases, meant you were funnier than everyone else. You just throw an F-bomb in front of every few words in a sentence and—

Bam!

You're the funniest kid in school. At least, that's what Sanjay and every other teenager in Oyster Shoals believed to be true.

Something was off this morning, and it wasn't sitting well with Sanjay. He looked up at the clock on his nightstand, it read 7:37 am.

Why was it so quiet? Usually his little sisters were already up and bouncing off the walls by now from some sugary breakfast item. Normally, he would have been drifting in and out of sleep due to being constantly awoken by their laughter, playful screams, or bickering matches. This morning was different, it was complete dead silence. Slowly, he got up from the bed and opened the door, making his way downstairs. He could hear the distant noise of what sounded like a kids cartoon show on the TV. He walked past the living room, peering in to investigate the situation. All that was there to see was the TV screen illuminating the room and furniture accents. *Ok, keep moving*, Sanjay thought to himself.

Eventually, he reached the kitchen and analyzed his family sitting at the breakfast table. His mom was reading the newspaper, and in the other hand, slurping up her coffee. His dad was doing the same, except gathering his news from his tablet. Sanjay always noticed his mom was much more old-fashioned than his dad. Sierra was staring down, looking depressed like she often did lately, her hair falling in front of her face, covering half of it. Sherpa was sitting there with her hands clasped while looking at each one of them at the table, Sanjay could tell she was studying them. Sherpa was a very observant kid, always studying people around her, trying to give every action and emotion they revealed a reason. They were all in their pj's still. For some reason, this always gave Sanjay a comforting feeling. He wasn't sure if it was the fact that he knew this meant they didn't have to go anywhere and could relax at home all day, or if it was something else.

Either way, Sanjay felt at home. Though he couldn't shake this feeling that his family didn't feel the same, or at the very least, Sierra. She'd been completely different ever since that day at the hospital. He almost felt like he didn't even know his sister anymore. *Maybe it was just puberty? Actually, I have noticed some zits on her face lately…all within her jawline area,* he thought. He had read this in one of those girly magazines once in the waiting room with his mom for a doctor's appointment. He remembered it had said the jawline area indicated hormonal.

Sierra watched her family as they all ate homemade blueberry pancakes. Blueberry pancakes were Sierra's absolute all-time favorite breakfast. With her stomach full of knots though lately, she couldn't even think about gagging them down. She was horrifically sick to her stomach ever since that incident in the forest. She felt as though her stomach was eating all the organs around it, then ultimately, turning on itself.

You traitor, she scolded her stomach. *I love food, especially blueberry pancakes, and because of you, I can't even eat, and if I do force some food down, I'll shit it out immediately. That's right, I said shit. All the cool kids are saying it now in the sixth grade,* she thought. She let out a deep heavy dramatic sigh, "Hhhuuuummm".

"You ok, Sierra?" her father asked.

"You ok, Sara?" Sherpa repeated inquisitively.

Sierra rolled her eyes and responded with a passive-filled, "Fine."

Jerry and Jovie both shot glances at one another. They were that couple that had that telekinesis thing going on. Jerry could see Jovie's face said, *what the hell was that?*

While Jovie could read Jerry's face that said, *well, I tried.*

Then they both gave each other a last look which displayed, *we'll talk about this later.*

"I'll help ya hunny, before I start work," Jovie said to Jerry, implying they go take care of the lifeless deer sooner than later.

"I wanna come with," Sanjay said.

"It's not going to be the prettiest sight, sweetie," his mom pointed out.

"But it needs to get done, right? Needs to be taken care of?" Sanjay tested.

Well, he certainly wasn't wrong, Jovie thought.

The three of them went stomping through the tall grass towards the gloomy chore.

"The deer is gone!" Sanjay exclaimed as he examined the situation before his parents reached the gruesome scene.

Jovie and Jerry gave each other that telekinesis glance again, this time their expressions said, *could this whole situation get any weirder?*

The whole situation had already been weird, currently was, and definitely was going to get weirder. As they got closer, all that was left was the skeletal remains of the deer.

"I mean, it's not that weird, a bear or mountain lion or some other animal could have devoured it during the night. Easy meal," Jerry said in hopes of defusing the worried vibes he was feeling. They went back inside the house, none of them feeling relieved by Jerry's comment, including Jerry himself. Quietly, the three of them sat back down at the breakfast table, not sure what to say or do next.

"That was fast," Sierra mumbled.

"Yea, well, it was easier than we thought," Jerry said as optimistically as he could.

"Der was no body, cause dat ding ate da deer," Sherpa said with a sticky face from the maple syrup. All of the Wintuk's faces except for innocent little Sherpa's went stone cold.

"Hunny, what do you mean by that?" Jerry questioned.

"I saw dat black ding with the pointy horns eating it last night," she said while putting her fingers on her head, imitating horns.

"Me and Boo—I mean, Boo and I were looking out da window at it," she sophisticatedly said, proud she corrected herself. Her family always corrected her when she would make that grammatical error. "It was scary, Boo didn't want to watch any longer, so we went under da covers. Den, it smelled weally bad, so we took the covers off and found pretty flowers on da bed," she responded.

Jovie felt her heart sink at Sherpa's comment. Felt her heart sink from her chest and drop down into the pit of her stomach like an anchor from a ship. Sherpa dug her chubby little hands into the pockets of her nightgown and pulled out a miniature bouquet of white flowers tied with brown frayed twine.

"Lily of the valley," Sierra said with a shaky dreadful voice.

"We need to call the police," Jerry blurted out sternly.

"Yea, because that worked out so great for us last time," Sierra murmured.

"Well, I don't know what else to do! Crazy shit is happening here and I don't know what the hell else to do, alright!" he began yelling defensively.

"I'll go grab my phone," Sanjay said while walking away. Sierra could feel her eyes begin to water, leaking out now like a broken faucet.

"Look, I'm sorry sweetie, it's just daddy's a little frustrated and worried right now. I'm sorry Sierra, sweetie," Jerry said while putting a hand on either shoulder, lowering himself to her eye level. She nodded her head at him, indicating she understood, looking up at him with big glistening eyes.

"I can't find my phone," Sanjay said.

"Ok, well go grab one of ours then, Sanjay. Please," Jovie responded, trying to remain polite under pressure. Sanjay reappeared after what felt like fifteen minutes or so.

"What took you so long?" Sierra snapped.

"I can't find any of the phones," he said with fear and confusion written all over his face.

"We have three phones in this house, you're telling me you can't find any of them?" Jerry asked. Sierra and Sherpa waited together while the rest of the family frantically searched the house for the mysteriously missing phones.

"Ouch!" Sierra yelped, "what was that for!" she questioned her baby sister.

"I jus needed to pinch you to see if we are dweaming or not Sara," Sherpa innocently replied. Sierra didn't reply, instead, she started thinking to herself that her baby sister's pinch test was pretty appropriate in a time like this where someone would hope they were just dreaming.

"Did da flowers taste like candy?" Sherpa asked, looking up at Sierra all wide-eyed and hopeful.

"What? No, Sherpa," Sierra responded with annoyance.

"*He* told me to eat dem, dat dey taste like candy," she explained. Sierra grabbed her sister, holding her chubby cheeks in her hands.

"Promise me, you will never ever eat those flowers. You will get very sick or die, do you want that? Hm? You promise me, never eat those flowers," Sierra solemnly said.

"I promise, Sara. Pinky promise," Sherpa said while holding her tiny pinky out to her sister. The two sisters held their pinkies out, interlocking them to bind this promise, then kissing the part of their exposed hands while interlocked still, sealing the deal.

After searching, the Wintuks met up in the kitchen; empty-handed again.

"All of the electronics are gone. Even my laptop," Jovie pointed out. She sounded winded, probably from a combination of stress and rummaging.

"Alright, grab some things everyone, we're leaving. Now!" Jerry directed while pointing a finger up the stairs that led to the bedrooms.

"Sierra, help your sister grab some things, please hunny," Jovie said with uneasiness.

Carrying bags and belongings, the Wintuks quickly got into their car. Of course, it was a Subaru Outback, complete with roof and rear racks. The residents of Oyster Shoals would consider this a stereotype, but you knew damn well if you lived in or were planning on living in O.S. (or some referred to as 'Overly Snobby'), you were getting a Subaru Outback sooner or later. It wasn't the best car for a family of five, but, priorities. However, the Wintuk's priority right now was to get out of there and get out of there fast. Like a typical scene from a horror movie, Jerry kept dropping the car keys from his shaking hands as he was trying to insert them into the ignition.

"Goddammit!" he yelled, obviously mad at himself for letting his clumsy emotions get the best of him. Jerry put the car in reverse and into drive quickly now, all of them getting jolted and jostled around in the vehicle that was too small for them.

"Why did we have to get this car!" Jerry yelled in frustration.

"It was the only type of used vehicle for sale around here, Jer!" Jovie yelled back. They squealed off and started making their way down the twisting turning road that would lead them out of the redwoods, back into town. The family only made it a mile or so out from their property until *he* appeared in the middle of the road.

He stood tall and powerful, *his* large overly muscular non-human like shoulders slightly slumped over, with his head hanging down. *He* cocked *his* head to the side and slowly looked up at them, his beastly horns appearing larger now as he peered

Up...

Up..

Up.

"Sherpa, don't look hunny!" Jovie yelled.

"I alwready seen *him,* member mama!" little Sherpa squealed back like a piggy.

"Stop trying to shelter her from the world all the time, Jove!" Jerry proclaimed.

"What? From the world? How many other fuckin' kids you think are seeing this shit right now other than ours! Huh!" she responded defensively.

Hypocrite, Sanjay thought to himself.

"Stop! Just stop!" Sanjay yelled at his parents, "look at *him*."

Jovie and Jerry cut short their debate and looked up at *him*, still standing in the middle of the road. *His* shiny solid onyx lips were curled back, revealing *his* sharp toothy smile. *He* appeared to have too many of those dagger resembling choppers in there, it was almost impressive that they all seemed to fit. *He* was breathing excitably, his nostrils flaring consistently from *his* bat-like nose. Jovie wasn't sure if it was just in her mind or not, but his pitch-black horns appeared to be getting longer, or maybe pointier? She really couldn't tell, it seemed almost like an optical illusion.

A car driving in the opposite direction appeared from the winding road that they sat in, surrounded by towering redwoods on either side. Before the driver could react in any way to *him* standing in the middle of the road, *he* picked up the car. Picking up the car with one claw, such ease and confidence oozed out of *his* deep pores from his obsidian skin. Plucking the driver out now, *he* chucked them against a tree, killing them instantly. A commotion could be heard, the Wintuks looked to their left and saw the half-naked horned people—or things—or whatever the hell they were. They were running on all fours out of the redwoods and to the now-deceased bystander who was just at the wrong place at the wrong time. The same could be said about the Wintuks. Though they still had a chance at survival, they weren't dead—at least not yet.

Chapter Four

He casually placed the car back down on the road, sitting on it with legs crossed. You could hear the crunching of the car from *his* abundant weight. *He* smiled curtly at them, putting one fist under *his* chin. Just then, a deer darted across the street, but *he* grabbed it, breaking its neck and one of its antlers off, throwing its body off into the woods. The half-naked creatures followed the inert deer into the woods like flies on shit. They were slobbering as they ran, the females breasts disturbingly dangling back and forth like saggy jowls on an old man. *He* smiled at the Wintuks again, almost sort of half-laughing to himself at how desperate the half-naked creatures must appear to them. *He* began using the antler he had broken off as a toothpick, nonchalantly maneuvering it around in between his teeth, or at least trying to, grinning at them as *he* did so.

"Pathetic, aren't they?" *he* inquired while nodding *his* head toward their direction. "Fucking maggots," *he* murmured from deep within *him*self. Somewhere dark within *his* soul, the darkest part of *his* abyssal soul. One might think a demon can't have a soul, but *he* did. A soul made up of rotting flesh and hand-picked parts of evil entities that no longer were among the living.

Jerry could feel his heart pounding so incredibly hard inside his chest, it felt like a ticking time bomb waiting to explode.

Tick-tock, tick-tock, tick-tock, tick-tock, pulsating through his heart's chambers. He didn't think it was possible to feel all four chambers, but he could clearly differentiate them now, *tick-tock, tick-tock, tick-tock, tick-tock…*

He could feel sweat forming profusely on his forehead, turning into liquid beads, before bursting and dripping down his face from excessiveness. A tide pool of sweat had developed on his upper lip, he licked his lips nervously and could taste his body's sodium, lingering on his taste buds. Jerry could feel his heart rate speed up as he examined and realized *he* was now mocking him. *He* was licking *his* lips, imitating Jerry but to much more extent, being overly dramatic. *His* tongue was far from anything human, it was like the tongue of a giraffe. It was an unnecessarily long purplish pale tongue. It was more than obvious *he* was taunting the family with it, trying to make them feel uncomfortable. *He* laughed arrogantly as *he* slithered *his* tongue up one nostril and slid it out the other, wiggling the tip sneeringly at them.

Then, *he* jumped abruptly up from *his* makeshift seat and placed a hand-like claw on either side of the road, lifting it, detaching it from the earth below. Then slamming it back down with great force, causing a huge wave effect. The road, now appearing as a black asphalt wave, was getting closer to them until all they saw was black nothingness.

Bam!

The car was soaring in the sky.

Craaaack!

It had roughly landed atop some redwoods, breaking some branches but not enough to break their fall. These redwoods were old and strong, with more years, came more trunk rings, and with more trunk rings, came a more stable tree. These redwoods varied anywhere between five-hundred to eight-hundred annual trunk rings, the most massive enormous redwoods probably in the United States.

Sanjay hazily woke up, still buckled up in the back seat. His head was throbbing with immense pressure like someone had been repeatedly slamming his head into the car window. Looking over to his right, he saw his baby sister had been pinned through her small chest by a branch, then looking past her, out of the other rear window, was Sierra, impaled on the top of a tree. His dad's head was drooped over onto the steering wheel, blood dripping down, while his mom had a gash in her throat from the broken windshield. Sanjay began to cry, or he had tried to but began choking instead. Coughing harder now, he could feel his eyes widen as he gripped his throat. His long eyelashes held drops of his hot tears, that even his frantic blinking couldn't make budge. Something was forcing his mouth open, he could feel something growing more and more out from his throat, scratching it along the way up. He glimpsed down and could make out white flowers—lily of the valley. He grabbed the stems with both hands and began pulling up and out, pulling, pulling, pulling…

Splat!

The soggy roots of the plant made a noise after he yanked it out, hitting the back of the driver's leather seat.

"Sanjay…Sanjay…," he could hear his name, it sounded far away though. "Sanjay…Sanjay…," he could hear it a little bit better now, sounding like it was getting closer. He couldn't open his eyes yet but was conscious. Staring at the inside of his eyelids, he could make out flickering pieces of natural light. It reminded him of staring up through the trees on a breezy day, the sun poking through every time the leaves swayed.

"Sanjay…Sanjay! Sanjay!" Jerry screamed, staring at his son through the rearview mirror. Sanjay awoke with a jolt, feeling his throat and wiping tears from his chin.

"Oh, Sanjay baby! Oh, thank God," Jovie exclaimed, touching her son's knee. He looked over to his right and saw both of his sisters were ok, scared and shaking, but alive and breathing, not impaled in any way.

He began sobbing, "I just had the worst nightmare. I thought you were all dead," crying harder now after saying the words aloud.

"It's going to be ok, sweetie. Good thoughts, ok?" Jovie said while turned around in her seat, staring at the three children. "We're not going to let anything bad happen to you. Ok? I know this is all very scary, and we don't know what's happening either, but we can't let our emotions get the best of us. We can't let those bad things get the best of us," she attempted to say in her calmest voice.

"How are we supposed to not let our emotions get the best of us? We are stuck inside of a car, that's stuck in a tree, that's stuck inside of a forest, with no one around, except for fucking creepy horned things!" Sierra screamed while sobbing.

"Watch it, Sierra," Jerry snapped.

"Yea, watch it Sara!" Sherpa shrieked with her cracking voice.

Sanjay leaned over Sherpa to put a hand on Sierra's arm, "Mom's right. I know you're really freaked out right now, but we all are. Freaking out isn't going to help or make anything better," Sanjay said reassuringly.

Thank you Sanjay, Jovie thought to herself. She smiled as she saw her son then move Sherpa's little head towards him, giving her a peck on the forehead.

The car began moving slightly, making the branches creak and bend.

Snap!

They all screamed as the car suddenly came to a falling halt onto another branch, landing lopsided this time.

"We need to get out of the car and onto the ground before this car comes crashing down with us in it," Jovie pointed out.

Sherpa began whimpering now, "I don't wanna go down where da scary dings are." She let out a baby pig squeal as another branch snapped, making the car fall some more.

"Hunny, we need to go—now," Jerry said with worry and a sense of urgency. He picked Sherpa up as she wrapped her arms and legs around him, stuffing her face into his neck, her glasses completely fogged up at this point. They all began crawling out of the car, grabbing onto surrounding branches and holding on tight.

Normally, Sierra would be significantly annoyed by now from the feeling of her palms and fingertips being tacky from the tree sap. This time though, she admired it's beautiful syrupy amber mess, oozing out between the bark. She stared down at her filthy hands, pressing her fingertips together and slowing pulling them apart, intrigued by it. About an hour ago all of this would be driving her crazy, but now, it didn't bother her one bit. At this moment, there was something almost comforting about it. She didn't know if it was the fact she was feeling something else physical other than a sore neck from the crash. Or, that the stickiness made her feel like she could grip onto the tree bark better. Or maybe, it was because she was feeling something that would have normally really bothered her, but now, it was so insignificant compared to all of this. It was so pointless. She started thinking about all the stupid small things that made her upset, and how meaningless it all was.

"C'mon!" Jerry yelled up to Sierra. "Snap 'outta it! Hold onto the tree for Christ's sake!" he said while snapping his fingers. She focused back into real-time, realizing her family was making their way down the tree, waiting for her to move with them.

"Coming!" she replied. After cascading the tree tactfully, the Wintuks all finally set foot onto the forest floor, except for little Sherpa who was still be carried by Jerry.

About an hour or so had passed by, "Sherpa, I gotta put you down, sweetie. My arms feel like they're gonna fall off," Jerry said to her while lowering the tiny girl.

As soon as her foot made contact with the ground, everything around her changed within the forest in an instant. Her family was no longer around her and the entire forest became crepuscular and hostile within a blink. She could feel her little heart beating so fast, pounding inside of her chest, as she glanced around in fear. Then the tears came,

came strewing down her soft baby-skinned face as she continued sobbing. The redwoods began oozing blood instead of sap, the crimson red-colored blood was profusely bleeding out, going into all the crevices between the bark. She looked down as the blood creepily descended the trees, following its movement now onto the dirt and mossy-patched covered forest floor. Sherpa noticed the ground started to slightly rupture where the blood had seeped onto, splitting open like a fault. Then, rising from the separation, pushing the earth out of its way, was a cluster of white flowers. She was surrounded now by lily of the valley plants, sprouting out from the miniature-like valleys they had created. She began frantically looking around as more and more of these flowers began rising from the bloody cracks in the earth.

Chapter Five

She must be exhausted, look at that daze. She looks like she's in a trance from being so tired, poor baby, Jovie thought to herself as she analyzed Sherpa walking along with them. Jovie picked Sherpa up since it appeared the little one was about to fall asleep while trotting along, her tiny legs wobbling back and forth.

"Mama!" Sherpa yelled while sobbing into her mom's shoulder.

"What is it, sweetie? I thought you were about to fall asleep. What's wrong?" she asked.

"Pwease don't put me down, someding bad happens," she said in her small quivering voice. Jovie and Jerry glanced at one another, they both felt that familiar significant other telekinesis kick in. They stared at each other for a sign, eyes moving back and forth, scanning for anything.

Their brains' engines were still warming up…*Aha!* Jerry thought to himself.

"What do you mean, sweetie?" he asked little Sherpa while stroking her soft hair. She went on to explain the terror she just experienced when he had set her down, and how it immediately stopped when she was picked back up. The Wintuks all couldn't help but realize they were walking through a place they all once loved so much, but now all seemed to hate. The crisp air—hate, sound of the trickling creeks—hate, the smell of the redwoods—hate, everything they admired before, they now couldn't stand.

"Ugh, it reeks of rotten eggs again," Sierra said annoyingly.

"Big surprise," Sanjay mumbled under his breath. They all covered their noses while trucking through the forest. The area they were walking in had prickly cucumber vines, spread out like veins across the forest, crawling up the trees, and hanging heavy over branches with their spiny egg-like fruits. You could hear the family crunching through the woods as they walked over a mixture of dried up pine needles and bark.

Jovie noticed her vision starting to become somewhat blurry, the voices from her family seemed to be drifting away and sounded so distant now in her head. She looked around and realized she was alone, standing there like live bait.

Shit, she thought to herself. *Shit, shit, shit.*

Something was moving from the corner of her eye, she glanced over to see what it was. It was a dangling prickly cucumber fruit. *Is it growing?* The fruit seemed to be doubling in size within seconds as it swelled up like a pregnant belly waiting to burst. The pointy spikes growing sharper and longer now too, protruding out from the oval abnormality. Leaning in to get a closer look, she could see through the now translucent sack from being so stretched out. Something was moving in there, wiggling around.

"Ah!" she yelped as a baby foot kicked the sack, you could see the outline of the foot through the thin layer. The surrounding hanging fruits all began growing, she slowly glanced around, confused and scared for what might happen next.

Pop!

Pop! Pop! Pop!

One by one, they all began bursting open, thick goo was covering her now, making her hair stick to her face as she stood there screaming.

"Waaaaaaaa!" could be heard echoing throughout the forest and pounding away at her eardrums. Jovie moved her plastered hair from her face as she peered up and saw the slime-covered newborn babies hanging from their umbilical cords. Dangling and swaying as they cried, crying that newborn baby cry. That kind of cry where you didn't even have to see the baby to know how new it is to the world, you just knew by hearing it.

Jovie slammed her hands over her ears and through streaming tears yelled, "What the hell do you want from me! Just stop!"

There *he* was. With the snap of his fingers, the cries stopped and the goo was gone. The hanging prickly cucumber vines were back to normal, it was as if none of that even happened. Jovie stood there trembling as she stared at *him. He* was sitting there on a lone tree stump in the middle of the forest.

"So Jove, how does it feel to have so many miscarriages? Do you feel like a baby killer? Not woman enough? Tell me, because I'm really curious, how does that feel?" *he* asked condescendingly, paired with hints of sarcasm. She couldn't open her mouth to speak, her body had gone numb due to shock. The way she felt reminded her of those dreams where no matter how hard you tried, you were incapable of screaming for help. She felt completely helpless. She began gagging now from how incredibly strong the rotten egg smell was, feeling it rise into her nostrils and spread to her mouth. She swore she could taste it.

"Oh, c'mon Jove, I don't smell that bad. Why does everyone think I smell so bad?" *he* asked while raising *his* arms into the '*I don't know*' motion and cocking *his* head to the side. The odor and taste was getting stronger, Jovie couldn't hold it in any longer and began vomiting, holding herself steady against a tree.

"Well, now you're just being dramatic," *he* said while crossing his legs curtly.

"Fucking drama queen," *he* scoffed while crossing *his* arms. She could hear the voices of her family filling her ears now, getting louder. *He* was fading away until completely gone.

————————

"Thank God!" Jerry yelled with relief. "We made it, Jove!" he exclaimed. She realized she was still carrying Sherpa, who had fallen asleep.

Was I walking this whole time? Looking over at her family, she could see how filthy and exhausted they all were. Twigs sticking out from their hair, rips in their clothes, and mud so heavily caked on the bottom of their shoes, probably adding an extra few pounds or so with every step. It was night now and she could see police lights flashing, coming to their rescue, she assumed.

"Good thing we found my phone!" Sanjay yelled excitably.

"What"? Jovie questioned.

"My phone," he said while holding it out now, "we found it in the woods, remember? Used it to call the police once we found a spot with reception."

Jovie didn't remember any of this, she didn't even remember walking, or realize she had been walking while carrying Sherpa this whole time. The last thing she wanted to do was scare her family or have them worry about her.

That's the last thing this family needed, she thought to herself. It was decided then, she would keep this to herself.

Sierra began crying tears of joy as soon as she saw those flashing police lights shine through the redwoods.

"Almost to the road! I see the lights!" she reassured herself and her family.

"Thank God!" Jerry said, alleviated. Sierra reached down to pinch herself. She pinched herself so hard with her nails that it drew blood.

Ouch! Wincing now as she rubbed the spot, nursing it. However, she had to be sure she wasn't dreaming. *We're saved*, Sierra thought to herself as a relieved smile melted across her face.

Sanjay didn't want to tell his family what he had experienced in the woods. Not only did he not want to worry them, but he was slightly embarrassed.

Is that the right word? Am I embarrassed? Am I insane? Why did it only happen to me? he started questioning himself. He embarked recalling what had happened to him earlier in the woods.

His horrid flashback began…

"Shhh," Sanjay said to his family as they trucked through the forest, "do you hear that?" They all stopped in their tracks and listened.

"What is that?" his father asked.

"It's my phone! It's around here somewhere!" Sanjay exclaimed.

"Huh? Isn't that the whistle song in *Kill Bill*, Sanjay?" his father asked with interrogation in his tone.

"Is that really important right now?" Sanjay responded while following the sound.

"Mom said you're not allowed to watch that movie," Sierra chimed in.

"Here!" Sanjay yelled while pointing down to a mound of fresh loose dirt. He bent down with an ear and could hear the song crystal clear now. With his bare hands, he dug into the dirt, feeling it tightly pack under his nails as he burrowed away. *Where the hell is it?* he thought as he slumped back, sitting on his heels.

The forest grew dim as he peered around, realizing he was now by himself, his family was nowhere in sight. Sanjay could feel something slithering over his ankles and tightening a grip. Thick tuber roots were rising from underneath the ground, cracking the surface of the forest floor. He began panicking and frantically flailing about like a fish out of water, but he soon discovered this made the roots move more quickly. "Help!" he screamed as he began crying. All he could think of at this moment was of a *National Geographic* show he saw once, where an animal was stuck in quicksand and all it could do was just wait. Wait for its time to go. He remembered how brave he thought the animal was, the look in its eyes said, *helpless but accepting.* It was admirable. He could feel the roots still crawling around his limbs, getting tighter, pulling him slowly down towards the earth's core.

Now just his head was above the surface, the smell and taste of soil and mother nature filled his senses.

The horned things appeared from behind the trees, walking towards Sanjay, now dropping onto all fours and inching closer to his head sticking out. They were sniffing him all over and drooling onto his face like a pack of hungry hyenas. One of the female's half-rotting grotesque breasts smacked him in the face as it swayed to and fro. Sanjay made a disgusted face as slimy drool dripped down his forehead. The horned things scattered as he heard a loud sudden—

Clap!

Looking up, Sanjay saw *him* standing there with claw-like hands clasped together.

"Animabus damnatis," he said deeply. Sanjay didn't know how to respond to this, continuing to stare at *him* like a deer in headlights. "That is what they are called. Not 'horned things', like you and your family keep referring them to," *he* pointed out.

Clap, clap!

Just like that, the forest became light again and his family was back.

"Here you go buddy," his father said while handing him his cell phone. Sanjay sat there, looking at his dirty hands, dumbfounded. "I don't know why you thought it was in the ground Sanjay, we wouldn't have been able to hear it that well if it were buried. It was laying over there," he said while pointing in another direction.

"What is his phone even doing out here?" Sierra asked while looking at her dad.

"I haven't the slightest clue, it seems this forest is full of tricks and mind games. All I know is we need to find service and call for help," he responded

while grabbing the phone from Sanjay now,
walking and holding the phone up towards the sky.

The flashback ended…

Chapter Six

The Wintuks decided to bury the whole haunting experience after that last day in the redwoods. Not once, did they even set foot again in those redwoods. They had hired a crew to go there and burn it down to the ground, belongings and all still inside. Shortly after that, an article was published in the local magazine, *Oyster Shoals Living*. It was titled, '*Has Jovie's horror novels finally gone to her head?*' The article went on about how even after someone offered her 6.8 million dollars for her newly built home, she still insisted on having it burned down. After residents of O.S. started speaking out amongst each other about the writer, a local journalist interviewed the police department. This article was about the officers' visit to the home after the deer incident, it was titled, '*Jovie's got a gun.*'

Clever, she thought.

"Reading '*Overly Snobby Living*' I see," Jerry said.

Jovie scoffed at this, saying, "Well, you know me, Jer. Reading the town's gossip about myself is one of my favorite pastimes."

"Things will get better," he said while kissing her on the head, "it's only been about five months, it's still fresh in their minds."

The family had moved to a suburban neighborhood this time around, within walking distance to the main beach. The Wintuks decided it would benefit them being closer to other people, living in an actual neighborhood, and hearing the usual noises. Garage doors opening and closing, trashcans going out every Tuesday night, cars honking and revving engines, obnoxious people talking on the phone through their car's Bluetooth speakers for all to hear; and the list goes on. Jovie didn't like any of this, she found most of it to be quite annoying.

But, at least we feel safer, Jovie thought to herself. The kids were also closer to their friends and could actually walk to school now too. Just then Jovie's phone vibrated, she quickly glanced down and could already see it was going to be one of those horrible memes she received now and then from her editor. She took a gulp of coffee, *Ok let's see what Naomi has to say this time*, she thought as she picked up her phone. It was a meme of a cat, looking down at a watch around its paw and it said, *'YOU BE DONE YET?'* She smirked and rolled her eyes.

Jerry glanced over at her, "What? What is it?" he asked.

Jovie responded, "I just think it's funny that even my editor gives into grammatically incorrect memes. I don't understand it. I don't get what the appeal is," she said while shaking her head and still smiling.

"I know what you mean, I saw one the other day that said, *'ME BE SO HUNGRY LIKE,'* and it had the cookie monster stuffing his face," he added. They both shook their heads at this.

Jovie began tearing the article up about her from the magazine, saying, "Yeah well me so over this shit."
Sanjay and Sierra both poked their heads into the kitchen, saying bye before walking off to school.

"Sherpa is still sleeping," Sierra informed her parents, as Jovie and Jerry both nodded at her, implying a 'thank you.' Sanjay and Sierra began their morning stroll to the only private school in O.S., that also happened to be the only Catholic school there as well. The only reason they went to this school was because of Jerry's religious background. This is where Jerry and Jovie stretched the rules a little bit in their marriage since Jovie was an atheist. Even though they had different beliefs, they loved each other unconditionally and kept the marriage strong through compromises. The compromise, in this case, was, if Jerry wanted them to go to this school so badly, then they didn't have to go to church every Sunday unless they wanted to do so and it wasn't done by force.

Sierra hated going to a school where she had to wear a uniform, it meant she had less opportunities to wear her favorite outfits. Sanjay on the other hand loved wearing the school informs. It meant he didn't even have to think about his clothing attire. It was one less thing to worry about for him. He even went through a phase where he was wearing his school uniforms on the weekends too. Thankfully he grew out of that phase, not to mention his uniform too since he had his biggest growth spurt yet during that time.

The one thing they were able to personalize was their backpacks. Of course, within reason, the school had a list of conditions you couldn't have on there. No affiliations with things such as sport teams, political views, certain organizations, blah blah blah—the list goes on. One time a student got in trouble for having a patch safety-pinned onto their backpack that said, *The Misfits*. Sierra remembered that poor kid's defense echoing through the halls, "It's a band! It's just a band!"

Though, it seemed the school didn't approve of this rock band.

Sierra had just added a new addition to her personal canvas—backpack that is. Jovie ironed the patch on for her the previous night and Sierra was over the moon excited to show it off the next day. The patch was simple, it read, '*My Clone Did It.*' It was humorous, and more importantly it made Sierra happy. Funny thing though, Sierra was such a goody-two-shoes that this would probably never apply to her, but regardless, it made her content. She was the Lisa Simpson of the family, at least that's what her parents would tell her all the time.

The two siblings were stopped at a crosswalk, waiting with a group of kids who were also on their way to the Catholic school.

"My clone did it," a kid announced from behind Sierra. She smiled to herself as he read it aloud, waiting for him to give an approving laugh or chuckle. "That's fucking stupid," he responded.

Another boy chimed in saying, "Laaaaame."

Sanjay turned around and snapped at them, "Leave her alone." The boys looked at each other, flabbergasted that this Indian kid just stood up to them. They both then proceeded to only talk to Sanjay with their best Indian accents, saying any racial slurs they could think of from their tiny thirteen-year-old minds.

"Why don't you go back where you came from?" one of them said snarlingly.

"Yea, why don't you just go back to India and your sister—friend or whatever, I mean you're not blood or anything. Why doesn't she just go back into a test tube?" the other one said in his best attempt to sound confident voice. No matter how confident this kid thought he sounded, he emitted insecurities. He could spit out a million insults and the Godzilla of slurs, and that wouldn't even touch on covering up all the insecurities this kid breathed.

Pow!

Sanjay turned around and socked one of the boys in the face. The boy covered his nose, bending down in pain, you could see drops of blood landing on the pavement. Sierra's defense senses kicked in now as she swung at the other boy with her backpack. She couldn't have picked a better day to load up her backpack with books to return to the school library. He was so caught off guard he fell completely back, making a hard landing.

His eyes were slightly watering as he looked up at her and yelled, "What the fuck was that for, Sierra?"

She casually pointed at the patch on her backpack, mouthing the words to him "My clone did it." Apparently, Sierra was capable of doing something where this would apply to her.

Sanjay and Sierra now both looked over at one another, "Run," he whispered to her. They both began running now, running as fast as they could. "Your backpack is too heavy Sierra, you gotta drop it," Sanjay pointed out to his sister.

"No!" she yelled back.

"Let me carry it for you then," he offered.

"No! Your just gonna get rid of it!" she accused, attempting to not sound too out of breath or tired from carrying the heavy load.

Sanjay glanced back and could see the boys attempting to catch up with them. They were moving slower, but now so were he and his sister.

"Ok, turn left up here. We're gonna go into that one coffee shop that's over there," Sanjay instructed her.

"What one coffee shop over there, Sanjay! There's like, five over there!" she yelled back. Panic consuming her vocal cords.

"The really hipster one. They won't do anything to us in a public place," he pointed out.

"They're all really hipster ones!" she said, obviously beyond annoyed.

"Fine! The one with the owl on it!" he yelled in frustration.

"I'm pretty sure at least three of them have owls!" she responded.

The two siblings made a hard left and Sanjay pointed out the coffee shop, "That one."

"Seriously? That's a Starbucks!" she said.

"Yea," he replied, winded from the escape taking place. She shook her head, rolling her eyes now as they approached the door.

"There's no owl on it either," she mumbled to herself.

They both slyly slipped through the doors, inching their way through the line and crowds of waiting grumpy people, yearning for their morning fix.

"Why did you have to choose this place?" she asked.

"Why not this place?" he questioned.

"It's too crowded, I never know where to stand. I always feel awkward," she explained.

"Look, just be a wallflower—like this," he said while suction cupping both palms and heels to the wall. He went as far as making suction cup noises when he did this.

"You look more like a starfish than a wallflower," she said back. Sierra took her brother's advice, trying to paste herself up against the wall as inpatient stares drilled judgments into them.

"Be one, with the wall," he said while closing his eyes. Sierra glanced over at him and could see him grinning, entertained by himself.

She giggled at his acting, "Uh huh, ok Ghandi," she responded.

"Ghandi? Stereotypes are a sign of weakness!" he said to her, trying not to break character.

"You know that's not what I meant, Sanjay! I didn't say it because you're Indian," she said.

He put an arm around her now, "I know, I know, I'm just giving you a hard time. No need to be so defensive," he assured her.

"Aren't you two supposed to be at school?" a random bystander asked.

"Aren't you supposed to be at work?" Sanjay replied. The conversation got cut short by a noise you knew was about to result in an accident.

Schreeeeeech!

Thunk!

The herd of people glanced towards the loud sounds, some even went running out to see what the commotion was. Sierra and Sanjay went to investigate now too, and to their surprise, and to be honest, somewhat delightful surprise, it appeared the two shit headed bullies were dead. They were crushed between a car and a building, the impact must have been so hard because their upper torsos fell over now, completely detached. The driver struggled to get out of their car.

A voice from the crowd yelled, "What the hell happened!" The driver looked severely distressed, not wanting to look at the aftermath, sobbing now in his shaking hands. You could hear all of the town's patrons concerned tones echoing throughout the streets.

Sanjay and Sierra then both listened to the driver say in a fearful voice, "It wasn't my fault, I swear. These horned things ran across the street…"

"You don't think—?" Sierra asked before being cut off by Sanjay.

"No, it can't be an animabus damnatis, we're out of the redwoods. Mom and dad said we're safe as long as we aren't there. Come on, let's get out of here," he responded. Sierra was the only person he had shared that piece of knowledge and horrifying experience with.

"Yea your right, it was probably just some other horned thing, like a unicorn," she said while glaring up at him.

"Well, Sierra, a unicorn and an animabus damnatis are about on the same level of fantasy for me," he said.

"Except one you've seen and the other you haven't," she pointed out. He ignored her as they kept walking, both picking up the pace and gripping onto their backpack straps tighter as their anxiety grew stronger.

"I miss our fort," she confessed with defeat.

"Me too," Sanjay agreed, "me too."

Chapter Seven

Living next door to the Wintuks was an elderly man, Angus Moray. He was somewhere in his eighties, very thin and frail, but still had a full head of hair probably due to good genes. He also had a Scottish accent, and if someone ever mistook it for being Irish, he would become extremely irate.

He would get red in his wrinkly face and start yelling, "Fur fuck's sake, I'm Scottish, goddammit. Th' accents sound completely different, an' I know how tah control mah liquor intake fur one!"—Or something close to that. Jovie enjoyed hearing him talk, it always put a huge smile across her face. While Jerry just absolutely couldn't stand the guy and constantly had to tell Sherpa that he wasn't a pirate. He chain-smoked Old Gold cigarettes like they were going out of style, even though they already were and had been for quite a while. In fact, he had to go to a tobacco outlet about an hour away just to get his smokes because no one in Oyster Shoals sold them. He would stock up on boxes and boxes of these damn cigarettes, storing them in a refrigerator in the garage. He insisted that this kept them fresh, dedicating that entire fridge only to store Old Gold cigarettes. Jerry also never saw the man drink anything other than black coffee.

He could recall a time when Angus's daughter was visiting the old man and she commented on how he should drink more water, he responded with a, "There's water in coffee."

No doubt, a stubborn old man, Jerry would often think to himself.

Jovie, Jerry, and Sherpa all sat at the kitchen table. This was their morning routine, Sherpa would come downstairs about half an hour after the two older ones left and sit with mom and dad. Depending on what phase of foods Sherpa was going through that week, it was either apple cinnamon oatmeal or sunny side up eggs on toast. She would tell her parents about all the dreams she had while Jerry watched the news on his tablet with one ear open, and Jovie loudly slurping up her coffee. Jovie had a horrible habit of slurping her beverages, though none of the Wintuks even took notice anymore since they grew so immune to the sound that most would find annoying.

"Yeah mama, you and papa were sheeps, and Sara and Sanjay were too!" Sherpa exclaimed.

"Well, what were you?" Jerry asked.

"I don't know atually…it was like a movie in my head," she said while pointing to her noggin. Jerry's tablet began ringing, making the kitchen table vibrate along with the silverware sitting on it.

"Whose that?" Jovie questioned.

"A number I don't know," he answered.

"It's prolly anoder sailor man," Sherpa announced. Jovie and Jerry both smiled at each other at this comment.

"I'm sorry Sherpa, it's probably another what?" Jerry encouraged.

"A sailor man!" she said.

"Oh…do you mean a salesman, sweetie?" Jovie implied. Yes, Sherpa meant a salesman indeed.

They could see Angus walking by outside from the kitchen bay window. The three of them stared and studied the old man as he hobbled up to his driveway with a cane.

"Look! It's a budderfly!" Sherpa exclaimed while pointing out towards the window.

"Oh yea, looks like a monarch!" Jovie chimed in as they sat there watching it flutter around the old man. He appeared distraught and bothered by the flying beauty, flailing his hand around dramatically and saying something probably inaudible to it. It landed on the cement driveway, just a few inches in front of him. He raised his cane and smashed the end of it right on the poor thing, smiling to himself after he did so. Angus was undoubtedly pleased with himself.

"No!" Sherpa cried out. She began crying, yelling and pointing, "You mean old pirate! You a mean pirate!"

Jerry and Jovie both stared at one another, jaws dropped and eyes that read, *What was that?* The two of them calmed Sherpa down and brought her into the living room to watch something more…happy.

Jovie and Jerry met up in the kitchen again, "What a miserable piece of shit," Jerry said.

"Seems like he's been more on edge lately, wouldn't you agree?" Jovie asked.

"I don't know Jove, I've never liked the man. I think he just needs to kick the bucket already," Jerry admitted.

Jovie knew something was different about Angus though. Sure, he's always been a little grumpy and outspoken since they've known him, but not evil. Not that killing a butterfly made someone evil, it's just that Jovie could tell something was different about him lately, something about his eyes. His eyes seemed beadier and suspicious now, and when you stared into them you immediately sensed lugubrious.

Jerry peered into the half-cracked open door of their study room, where Jovie was working, or at least trying to. She kept getting distracted by her thoughts, which led her to sit in that room for over two hours without even completing one full sentence.

"Jove," he said.

"Jer," she responded wittingly.

"I'm going to pick the kids up from school, just got a call that they're being let out early today. Two students died this morning. Got hit by a car while walking to school. They have counselors at the school right now if any of the kids need it," he said to her in a sorrowful tone.

"Oh my God! Well, who—?" she said while covering her mouth.

"I don't know, they said they couldn't say yet. Just relieved it wasn't Sanjay and Sierra," he said.

"I'll come with you," Jovie responded.

"Hunny, Sherpa just went down for a nap. I'll just pick them up real quick and we'll be back in no time," he said assuringly. Now for sure Jovie wasn't going to make any progress on her writing that day. She immediately started looking up online for any information regarding the accident. Every article she clicked on though was short and vague, offering very little to no information. She even started calling some of Sierra and Sanjay's friends' parents to see if they had any information, not to mention that hopefully, it wasn't one of them since she knew a lot of them walked to school also. All of the parents reported the same thing to Jovie, no one knew or had answers. The sound of the front door could be heard opening, Jovie got up from her chair and briskly made her way downstairs. She hugged the two of them and kissed both of their foreheads.

"Oh, I'm so relieved it wasn't you two that it happened to," she whispered as she squeezed them harder now.

"It was Brian and Victor," Sierra mumbled.

"Huh?" Jovie questioned now while looking them both in the eyes.

"That was their names," Sanjay answered.

"I thought no one knew who it was yet except for immediate family? Even the news isn't saying," Jovie responded. Sanjay and Sierra both quickly glanced over at one another, trying to think of how to respond to mom's observation.

"I-I-mean, everyone at school knows. All the kids know. It's-it's all everyone is talking about. It's a known thing," Sanjay spurted out as nonchalantly as he could.

Jovie gave them both a confused look, now shooting Jerry a telekinesis look that said, *something is fishy here.*

"What?" Sierra asked her mom.

"I had made some phone calls to some of your friends' parents and they all said the same thing, including the school faculty too," she said while piercing daggers into their pupils with her stare. Sierra could feel her face turning red and her heart rate spike in that moment as she stared back at her mom. Trying to look as calm and collected as possible, even though she felt like she could burst at any second as she felt her mouth nervously twitching.

Why did I have to open my big mouth, she thought to herself. Sanjay stared back into his mom's eyes as he kept anxiously blinking his eyes to an unnecessary extent. He also had a nervous habit of rubbing his nose as if he had a quick itch on it constantly.

Why did Sierra have to open her big mouth, he thought to himself.

Just then a local news reporter could be heard from the TV that was on in the background, "With permission from the parents, photos of the two children who lost their lives today in a tragic accident involving a reckless driver. May you rest in peace." The Wintuks gathered to the living room to find three photos on the TV screen, two young boys with the names Brian and Victor underneath them, and the third of a disheveled looking man that said, Peter - Reckless driver. Jovie and Jerry glanced over at Sanjay and Sierra.

Sanjay quickly added, "Yea, I mean everyone was talking about it right as dad was picking us up. I'm assuming it was breaking news. You know, one person told another, and another, and it just started spreading from then on. I'm assuming," he added again with a silent but bulbous gulp.

Chapter Eight

Two weeks had gone by and nothing too out of the ordinary happened. The only thing that came to Jovie and Jerry's mind was the fact that Sherpa kept having the same reoccurring nightmare every night.

A disturbing dream for a four-year-old to have, Jerry thought to himself every morning while he heard her tell it again. In this dream, Sherpa would wake up in the middle of the night and walk over to her bedroom window that faced the backyard. She would lookout to see the neighbor, Angus, sitting there, half-naked at one of those cheap white plastic patio sets. If you saw it, you would know exactly what kind of cheap white plastic chairs and table she was trying so hard to describe to her parents. He was sitting there with one leg resting on the other, chair aimed at her window, only wearing adult diapers, and just staring while smoking a cigarette. The smoke appeared to be drifting in slow motion, never really fully dispersing, just sort of seemed to be smoke layering on top of more smoke. He looked like he was sitting in his own filth while it polluted the air all around him. The naked parts of his body had open sores scattered about, appearing wrinkled and pale like a used napkin, that should have been thrown out countless uses ago. He would just stare at Sherpa looking out her window, emotionless, almost like a statue. Only then in the dream she would realize he could move when he'd raise the cigarette to his mouth to suck in another hit, watching the tip get brighter as he sucked, slowly dimming as he released. He would slide down, out of the cheap plastic chair, and slither like a python towards her window. Then, the dream would end with just the two of them staring at each other, and soon after Sherpa would really wake up.

This particular morning, Sherpa awoke like usual after the older two left for school. She stretched a big stretch and yawned a cute small yawn, her mouth smirking to the side as she did so. Rubbing her sleepy eyes, she pitter-pattered over to her bedroom window and peered out. She could see Angus in his backyard, standing in the middle of his yard with one hand on his cane. His back was to her so she took this opportunity to continue to stare, studying him closely.

What is he staring at? As if he could sense her fixed eyes burning into his back, he turned around to face her. He waved at her. She did what probably any four-year-old would do and returned the greeting. Then, he bent his other fingers so that just his index finger was pointing up. Pointing it proudly up, he displayed it to her as if he was going to do a magic trick, even making '*oooh*' and '*aaah*' faces at his finger. Curious as Sherpa was, she continued watching, almost feeling sort of intrigued now, she couldn't wait to see what was going to happen next.

Then, he jammed his finger up his nostril, burrowing around inside of there, picking his nose the hardest Sherpa has ever seen anyone pick their nose. It started to scare her as he began getting violent now, even what she believed to be blood started dripping out. Pulling his finger out, he displayed it to her again and inserted it into his mouth, sucking anything that was on his finger off. She watched as an excessive grin took over his entire face, his high cheekbones framing the vexing sight. He waved at her once more.

Sherpa began crying and ran as fast as her little feet could downstairs to her parents in the kitchen.

Bam!

She ran right into mom's ass as she took a sharp turn into the kitchen, slipping in her socks on the smooth glossy wood floors. Thereupon, she bounced back from the impact and readjusted her glasses—that surprisingly haven't broken yet.

"She always does that," Jovie said to Jerry while bending down to pick up baby Sherpa. She moved her daughter's hair out of her wet slobbery face, asking now, "What's wrong baby girl?

"Huh? What's wrong, sweetie?" Jerry asked as he got up from his seat and laid a comforting hand on Sherpa's back.

"The pirate! I hate him!" she screamed while pointing up towards the stairs.

"Another dream?" Jerry asked her.

"No, dis time it was wreal!" she responded while sobbing into her mom's neck. She explained to them what happened and both Jerry and Jovie were disturbed by this to say the least.

Jerry walked over to the front door, opening it up with authority, while saying, "I'm going to have a word with this son of a bitch." Jovie gave him the telekinesis head nod of approval that also said, *good luck to you hunny.*

———

Bang, bang, bang!

Jerry waited a few more seconds.

Bang, bang, bang!

Stupid miserable son of a bitch, he thought to himself. He could hear the old man making his way to the front door.

Bang, bang, bang!

"Pipe doon! I'm comin'!" he yelled from the other side of the door.

I'll show you pipe down, I'll grab one of your bagpipes and shove it up your old loose ass, Jerry thought to himself as he heard the unlocking of the door. Angus opened the door with just the screen now separating them, "I need to have a word with you," Jerry said in a stern, yet polite tone.

"Come in," was all Angus said back. Jerry could tell the inside of the house was dark and barely lit even through the screen door. He walked in and glanced around, really examining the place since this was his first time stepping foot in there.

There were some tall candles lit, hot wax streaming down them onto various parts of furniture that he obviously wasn't worried about or cared enough for. The whole house seemed to be lightly smokey inside, consistently rotating and whirling lazily around in the stagnant and stuffy air. Every surface Jerry looked at appeared to be covered in coffee mug rings, some stained, and others were not bothered to be cleaned up. Every piece of furniture that had fabric on it was littered with cigarette burns, as well as the carpet too. Multiple items in the house were visibly discolored due to smoking indoors. What appeared to be black tar was caked onto parts of the walls, ceilings, door and window frames. *I can only imagine what his lungs must look like*, Jerry thought.

They entered a dining room where Angus sat down, stuffing a grimy cloth napkin into his shirt

and motioning to the chair across from him, "Sit,"
he instructed. Jerry looked down at the chair's
fabric seat, feeling his mouth become overly dry as
if the house itself was sucking the life out of him.

"Oh c'mon, sit. Th' fag burns won't bite," he
joked. Jerry bit his tongue and forced his body to sit
down across from the old scummy man, his face
twitching now as his OCD tendencies kicked in.

Fuck, fuck, fuck, he thought to himself
repeatedly in his head.

"Ye ever hud haggis before, Joseph?" Angus
asked.

"My name is Jerry," he corrected the old bastard.

"Do ye know whit tis made of?" Angus
continued. Jerry decided to not answer at this point,
as he continued staring at the gross old man and all
of his distracting liver spots. "It's a combination of
suet, oatmeal, sheep's heart, liver, an' lungs.
Encased an' cooked inside ay' th' sheep's stomach.
It's illegal in th' U.S., but I hae mah ways, Joseph,"
he said. Jerry didn't even bother correcting him this
time. "Its like cashmere on th' tongue," he went on
to describe. Angus picked up a knife and sliced the
sheep's stomach open, letting the haggis fall out
from inside of it, watching it pour out onto a plate.
"So, do ye want tae be a sheep or not be a sheep?"
Angus questioned Jerry, staring up at him with
vainglorious eyes as he stuffed a handful of haggis
into his mouth, and a finger up his nostril. He began
hysterically laughing now, saying, "Some like one
in th' hole, Joseph!"

"That sick fuck!" Jerry yelled while storming back into the house. Jovie ran over to him with worried eyes.

"What happened, Jer?" she asked while laying a hand on his shoulder.

"He's fuckin' sick in the head, Jove. I don't even want to talk about what just happened right now. I'll tell you later. Where's Sherpa?" he asked.

Jovie seemed a little put-off but also understanding of her husband's request, "She's watching TV," she responded.

"I don't want any of the kids talking to that man or even looking at him. He's not just the funny grumpy old man anymore, Jove. He's changed. He's sick," Jerry explained. They both agreed on this new rule and made a pact to sit down with the kids later on to voice their concerns.

"You think we should contact his daughter?" Jovie inquired.

"Well…," Jerry had to think about it for a second or two, "that's not a bad idea. Perhaps we should reach out to her. Tell her that he may be sick, and seems to be getting worse," he added.

The following day they both did some research and found his daughter's contact information, her name was Lexi. From what they could tell online, all indicators pointed to her living somewhere in France. She looked to be somewhere in her late forties, maybe early fifties. A very large woman she was, with shiny rosy puffed up cheeks.

"She sort of reminds me of a pufferfish," Jerry said to Jovie as they both stared at the computer screen. Jovie looked over at him and rolled her eyes. "Yeah, look at her Jove, it's like every time she smiles, she puffs up. Now, look at this picture here of the specimen not smiling. Here, she is…well, deflated," he said to her in his best commentator voice. Jovie tried hard not to laugh at this, hiding her face as she slurped her coffee up loudly.

"Ok, Jer, we need to focus," she pointed out while holding in laughter, trying to sound serious and professional.

"Right," he said, looking down solemnly. "We must now call the pufferfish!" he exclaimed while pointing a finger up. She spit out her coffee, letting her laughter escape now.

"Look what you made me do, Jer!" she yelled while still giggling. Jovie had called and left Lexi a voicemail, as well as emailed the three different email addresses she found for her online. "Well, now we wait," Jovie said aloud.

Chapter Nine

"What happens to a frog's car when it breaks down?" Sierra asked her family while reading from a sheet of paper. They were all sitting on the couch as her audience while she did her stand-up comedy bit.

"Um…it hops?" Sherpa squeaked.

"Noooo," Sierra responded while shaking her head.

"Oh I know! The answer has something to do with Frogger!" Sanjay exclaimed proudly.

"No! It gets toad away!" Sierra announced. They all began to laugh, Sherpa not really getting it but laughing along because she didn't want to be left out.

"Dat's funny, Sara!" Sherpa yelled, looking at her parents and Sanjay for approval. The yearly talent show at the Catholic school was approaching. Every year Sierra would sing, but this year was going to be different, she wanted to do stand-up comedy. She had compiled a list of jokes and puns to read aloud to her family in the evenings to see which ones seemed to be the funniest and most popular among them. After weeks of doing this, Sierra knew which jokes she was going to keep and remove.

"My final list of jokes is now complete," Sierra said nobly.

"By Jove, I think she's got it!" Jerry yelled while putting an arm around Jovie. Sierra still didn't know why her dad always said that to her mom, but they would always smile at each other afterward.

Sanjay didn't have time to be part of the talent show since he was busy with the school's swim team; or at least that's what he always used as an excuse. Every Friday, the swim team would go down to Urchin Cove and practice their laps there. It was Sanjay's favorite exercise they did, not only because it was different from the everyday pool, but after they completed their laps, they had free time. During free time, Sanjay would usually body surf or dive under waves with his friends. He loved floating atop the curling waves, right before they crashed down. As he rose to the highest point on the wave, he would stare down at the steepness that ultimately would plummet you down into it's curled mouth if you didn't continue floating onto the other side. Looking at how small everyone appeared at the shoreline, he would wave as if he were the king of the ocean when he was at the tip-top point of his liquid throne, which would then cradle him down and back up again.

It was Friday at Urchin Cove and Sanjay was in the water like usual, going up and then down over the towering tall slick waves. He smiled as he floated over the steep waves, looking at the ant-sized people on the sand.

Up and then down...

Up and then down...

What was that? He had already gone back down, the backside of the wave was blocking his view.

Going back up now...*Him. He* stood beyond the shoreline, in the cypress tree grove. Stood there not moving, just staring at Sanjay with *his* red eyes from a distance.

Floating back down...

He began to pant, breathing harder now, noticing the pressure on his chest from the water that never seemed important or bothersome before.

Going back up…*Where was he?*

Going back down…

Going back up…back down…back up…back down…

up…down…up…down. *I don't see him.*

Down!

Down!

Down!

Sanjay frantically glanced around while he was being pulled under and into the deep ocean. Looking below, towards his feet, he could see thick kelp was wrapped tightly around his ankles, pulling him down further. He could feel the water temperature dropping drastically as he got dragged down through the kelp forest, his body started feeling icy as goose-bumps formed on his skin. The kelp forest he was surrounded by appeared to be coming alive, the seaweed moving unnaturally, not just with the current. It seemed to have a mind of its own, wrapping around Sanjay and tugging him around. He looked towards the ocean floor and saw it covered in purple sea urchins and orange starfish. It was beautiful.

Why was something so horrible happening in such a beautiful place? Is this how death appears to the one who's dying? Horrible, yet beautiful at the same time? Sanjay thought all these things to himself as he admired the scene around him. It was like his mind had entered a state of calmness and acceptance, just like the dying animal he saw on *National Geographic.*

Everything went black.

———————

Sanjay woke up in a hospital bed, surrounded by his family and vases of flowers.

"Oh!", his mom yelped with hope as she covered her mouth and held his hand. The next half an hour or so was full of joyful cries, hugs, and kisses from his parents and sisters. Sanjay soon learned that he had been in a coma for a week, but he felt as though that whole incident at Urchin Cove happened only an hour ago. His sense of time was completely thrown off. Not to mention, he had also learned that he was brought to the hospital for drowning due to what the lifeguards assumed was the result of a large wave.

Later on, before Sanjay was allowed to leave, he heard the doctor make a comment to his parents about, "Keeping us kids out of trouble." Then, chuckling afterward, like he thought he was so clever for making that connection. Sanjay didn't think it was that out of the ordinary for him and Sierra to both have ended up in the hospital at some point during the last year.

I hate that guy, Sanjay thought to himself as the doctor patted him on the head and said, "You listen to your parents now mister and stay out of trouble, you hear?"

Yeah, well, you're not getting tormented by a fucking demon now are you? Sanjay thought to himself as he glared up at the man's stupid grin. At least that's all Sanjay could think, *he*—could be. *He* must be a demon, Sanjay conversed in his mind. *He* must be.

———————

One week had gone by.

"Today is the big day!" Sierra yelled excitably as she ran downstairs, skipping the last few steps so she could jump down, like this was making a statement, or just for pure fun. Jovie and Jerry didn't even have to see it happen to know that's exactly what she did as they heard the thump of her landing. She skidded into the kitchen, removing her backpack and setting it on the table, handing her mom a new patch.

"Can you please iron this one on for me before we leave for school?" Sierra asked her mom with big pretty please eyes.

"Of course, sweetie," Jovie responded. The patch was of a venus fly trap plant and above it read, '*Bite Me.*'

Jovie began her daughter's request as Jerry poured them both some more coffee, saying to Sierra, "I like the new addition, it's funny" as he looked up, smiling at her.

"Thanks, dad," she said as a bashful smile dispersed across her face.

With the new patch ironed on, Sanjay and Sierra were on their way out. Gazing out the window, Jovie watched as Sanjay walked with both hands grasping his backpack straps, head down, and Sierra skipping in front of him.

"He seem ok to you?" Jovie implied with a head nod towards Sanjay, looking over at her husband.

"It's hard to tell. Sometimes I'm not sure if something is bothering him or if he's just going through the motions of being a typical teenager," Jerry responded.

"Oh, I meant to tell you, Jer. She emailed me back—Lexi," Jovie informed.

"Oh? The pufferfish has responded, you don't say?" he said while raising his eyebrows.

She smirked back, "Yes, Jer. The pufferfish has made contact."

Jovie went on to tell him about the long and unnecessarily detailed email from Lexi. "The bottom line is, she's not surprised and has been expecting this for some time now. I haven't gotten a for sure answer from her yet, but it sounds like she's planning on coming out here sooner than later," Jovie said.

Well, good, maybe we'll get lucky and his daughter will move him outta here, Jerry thought to himself. As he ended that thought he could feel someone looking at him. Jerry gazed up out the window and saw Angus poking his head out between his curtains, glaring at him, then retrieving his head and slamming them closed. Jerry scoffed, shaking his head at how ridiculously miserable the old man was.

———

Later on that evening, Jerry, Jovie, Sanjay, and Sherpa started walking to the Catholic school to watch Sierra's performance. It was a breathtaking night, the air was cool but not cold, with a light refreshing breeze that smelled of salt and cedar. The streets were still wet from the gentle rain they had earlier in the day, but the skies had cleared up now. Sherpa loved staring at the glossy asphalt streets at night after it had rained. The reflection from the streetlights always appeared smeared across the slick streets, reminding her of an oil painting. They walked up the stone stairs to the school's large double doors, with an enormous cross mounted to the roof that hung above them. As Jovie walked she peered up at the cross, cringing a little but doing her best to hide it, while Jerry smiled at the sight and felt relieved. Sherpa skipped through the doors not phased by anything.

Sierra was backstage with the rest of the performers, the hustle-bustle of everyone getting ready in front of their lit up mirrors was still going on as you could hear the announcer talking on stage. She could hear the announcer making a corny joke referencing the rain they had earlier that day.

"So, the weather baptized all of us today, am I right?" he asked as the crowd laughed and cheered. "Yes, it was a blessed day, and still is for that matter!" he added.

Sierra sat there, looking at herself in the mirror, then looked around to see what the other girls were doing at this time, feeling sort of out of place. Fellow girls were putting on eyeliner, powdering their young faces, and chatting amongst one another with one hand on a curling iron. All curling their hair at once and freely moving the other hand about as they spoke, making it all look so easy. She watched them as they went to one another, asking and taking turns zipping each other up.

"Hi, um, would you mind helping me?" she asked one of the girls standing in a group. The girl and her two other friends looked at one another, indicating they thought this was weird and were definitely going to gossip about Sierra later.

"Ummm, sure. What do you need help with? Doesn't look like you need a dress zipped up," the girl said.

The two other ones began giggling. Sierra held her arms out to the girl, "Could you please button my sleeves?" she asked. Her plaid shirt had an area where once rolled up to the desired location, the button could be fastened, insuring your quarter length sleeve would stay put. The girl began buttoning without saying a word. Once the girl finished fastening her sleeves, Sierra thanked her. All she got in response though was an eye roll followed by an empty sounding, "Yeah."

Sierra watched as another girl started applying lipstick, analyzing her technique. She reached into her backpack and pulled out chapstick, applying it to her lips in the same manner. Pulling out her list of jokes that she already had memorized, she began studying them once again, implanting the sequence of her jokes into her mind.

Almost there, Sierra thought to herself as she sat patiently and nervously waiting. She began shaking her right leg now with anxiety, bouncing it up and down. If her mom were there right now, she knew this would be the moment where she would rest her hand on her knee, look over at her and mouth, "Stop." At this thought, Sierra put her sweaty palm on her knee, trying to settle it down, taking one deep breath in and a deep exhale out. Now she could feel her butt sweating with fear.

Dammit, I hate when my butt sweats, she thought to herself, her leg shaking starting up again. The only time her butt sweat was when she had to do anything that involved public speaking. She hated public speaking but wanted so badly to do her stand-up comedy bit, and not just in front of her family anymore.

One performance was ending, as the announcer was getting ready to say the next act. The next act was Tony Charter. Sierra made her way to the stage wings, preparing herself to go on soon.

He's the last person right before I go up! She thought to herself with butterflies in her stomach. Her eyes began to water with pure excitement and nervousness.

Tony walked by her as he made his way to the stage, leaning towards her ear and saying into it, "Girls can't be funny, Sierra." She was confused by his comment, speechless and utterly dumbfounded, not really even knowing what just happened.

She pinched herself, *Ouch!* she thought as her body flinched. *Not dreaming.*

She watched from the side of the stage, as Tony's mouth formed the words, "What happens to a frog's car when it breaks down?" Pausing now, "It gets toad away," he answered. The whole audience began laughing and clapping now, Sierra looked at her parents and she could see them both giving each other confused expressions. He continued with more jokes, Sierra could feel her face get hot as her legs became numb as she began to realize he had stolen her act. Every single joke he was saying was in the exact order as hers. He bowed as his performance came to an end, the audience clapping and whistling for him. He grinned at Sierra, walking past her and mouthing the word, "Thanks."

Chapter Ten

"Now, Sierraaaaa Wintuk!" the announcer yelled. She unzipped her backpack, pulling another piece of paper out from it, this time it wasn't the list of jokes, but a sheet of music. "Sierraaaa Wintuk!" she heard the announcer yell again, hinting at her to come on stage. She forced her legs to move as she approached the microphone in the center, handing the announcer the sheet of music.

"Oh, umm, I guess Miss Wintuk has decided to sing a song instead!" he announced while handing it off to the large woman on the piano. Sierra stood there with her head down, looking up now to see *him* standing in the back of the audience. *His* enormous arms were crossed with *his* long nails dangling, as *he* peered up at her with those red eyes and solid black irises. *His* heavy horns protruded from *his* head, almost touching the ceiling.

"I'm singing *'I Love You, God,'* written by anonymous," she said quietly into the microphone. Patrons in the audience all gave each other pleasing looks, expecting their ears to be filled with hallelujahs and praises to the Lord, while her family gave each other concerned glances. The piano started as the audience smiled approvingly and Sierra began to sing.

"Did you make the stars and the moon?
The ocean's current and the sun shining too?
The colors displayed at sunrise and sunset,
I bet you made them all, didn't you?

I love you, God,
Is what I would have said before,

But I don't believe in you, God,
I believe you are just a lore,
That humans made up, to fill in voids

For if you were real, God,
We wouldn't argue about our beliefs in which God
is the one,
We wouldn't pray to you and thank you for
meaningless things,
Sports victories, money, fame, and acne to go away
Come the morning sun

If you were real, God,
You would answer the crucial prayers,
Dying children, diseased humans, malnourishment,
and rapes,
When you think about it, God,
Why should someone have to pray to you for you to
jump in and help?
Is the two-year-old child who gets raped and
abused daily
Supposed to accept the cards they've been dealt?

I love—"

Booing could be heard throughout the building,
people began yelling to take the girl off stage. Some
parents were covering young virgin ears, while
others were getting up to leave. *He* swung his hand
down, making the ground crack and spread apart.
Like a strong unseen force, people were thrown
back into their seats, unable to move or even blink.
The woman on the piano continued to play out of
intimidation. *He* looked at Sierra, motioning his

hand for her to continue, his smile spreading like a deep fault in his face, drool dripping slowly down.

"I love you, God,
Is what I would have said before,
But you're not even real,
What else do you have for us in-store?
Another war, holocaust, or segregation?
Perhaps more hate crimes, suicides, and shootings
of children?

Pray to God, he will make everything better,
Is the biggest lie of them all,
No bullies or beatings will stop after a prayer to
God,
No drug addictions and shooting up behind a
bathroom stall

Did you sin and now you're afraid of going to Hell?
It's ok, as long as you confess to them,
All is well
The babies you killed, the humans you
dismembered, the school you shot up,
The people you raped, the kid you bullied until no
sound,
It's all ok because you have confessed now

God doesn't hold a plan for you
Because he doesn't exist,
You hold a plan for you
Call me a pessimist

I love you, God,
Is what I would have said before
But I don't believe in you God

Not anymore"

He was clapping *his* long claw-like hands in approval while the rest of the audience cried and shouted as they were glued to their seats by the diabolical force. Suddenly, the cries slowly started turning into cheers, and the faces in the audience were no longer in distress but looked overly happy and gleeful.

"Bravo! Bravo!" *he* bellowed deep from within as *his* teeth glistened and *his* nostrils flared. The entire audience began throwing bouquets of white flowers to Sierra on stage. Showering her with bouquets made up entirely from lily of the valley flowers.

He inhaled, looking up at Sierra, "They smell so sweet, don't they, Sierra?" *he* asked.

Splash!

Sierra awoke from water being splattered on her face. It reminded her of the time her parents had her baptized, except this was no baptism she thought to herself as she blinked repeatedly and rubbed her eyes. Apparently, Sierra passed out backstage after Tony Charter's comedy bit; well, supposed to be her comedy bit. The piano lady was leaning over her, putting a pillow under her head, but had basically stuffed Sierra's face into her bosom while she was at it. Sierra's face was being squished harder as the woman maneuvered the pillow under her head, lifting her neck. Piano lady pulled away now after proper pillow placement was satisfactory and Sierra could breathe again.

Goddamn, woman! Sierra thought as she gasped for air.

Her parents rushed backstage and leaned down, telling her not to move or get up, "Just take it easy, Sara," Sherpa said, mimicking her dad's instructions.

Sierra could hear the piano lady in the background saying, "She must have let her nerves get the best of her and passed out." At that moment, she could feel Sanjay's gaze on her. Similar to their parents, they had the sibling telekinesis thing going on.

Sanjay's stare said, *I know there's more to this, and we're going to talk about it later.* While Sierra's look said, *you got me, and yes, I'm fully aware.*

Sierra felt depressed the whole weekend, no amount of words of encouragement or silly iron-on patches from her parents could turn her mood around. Sierra didn't tell her parents what Tony Charter said to her, but she did tell them that he stole her jokes. Or yet, her parents pried that information out of her since they knew it was too much of a coincidence and brought it up to her. Of course, she began sobbing as soon as they brought it up.

Parents were always so good at that, anyone else could ask, "What's wrong, Sierra?" And she could easily hide her true emotions and display her best poker face.

However, it was a whole other story when her parents looked her in the eye and asked, "What's wrong, Sierra?" It would always start with her eyes watering, her bottom lip quivering, followed by a golf ball-sized lump in her throat throbbing, just wanting so badly to spurt out. Then, her cries and tears would come pouring out like something inside of her had just broke or malfunctioned. She hated having zero control sometimes, but, she was only human.

Sanjay ended up telling Sierra everything that happened to him on that horrific Friday at Urchin Cove. As well did she tell him the full story of everything that happened to her at the talent show. They both cried, which was reassuring but also made it all too real, at least that's how Sierra felt. Sanjay on the other hand was debating on if they should tell their parents or not. He knew his parents were dealing with some adult crap, whatever that was— but he knew they were based off evenings of eavesdropping to the tones of their tongues. He didn't want to give them more to worry about or for the press to catch wind of any of it. The articles about his mom had just come to an end, he couldn't even remember the last time he saw or heard a rumor or piece of gossip about his mother. It was old news now in the public's eye, the last thing they needed was an article that read, '*Author, Jovie Wintuk's family has gone crazy too!*'

Chapter Eleven

Knock, knock, knock!

Jesus, Jovie thought to herself. *Who the hell bangs on a door like that?*

"Is that necessary?" Jerry said while looking at her.

"You read my mind," she mumbled to him.

Knock, knock, knock!

It sounded like an ogre was banging on the door with its mighty fists, banging away until it got what it wanted. Jerry got up and answered the door, now face to face with a disturbingly obese woman and a stoic stare. Her eyes reminded him of charcoal lumps, and she had a long pointy nose resembling a carrot, even the tip was slightly crooked. He immediately pictured her as a snowman—er snowwoman, after realizing this comparison and smiled to himself.

"Jovie here?" she asked in a dark brown voice. No, her name was not Lola. In fact, this was Lexi.

Jovie intervened from behind Jerry, poking her head from around him, saying, "Hi, Lexi?"

Lexi responded masculinely, "Aye, that would be me. Ah know, ah look much different now…then before. Doctors hink ah may, em, have a thyroid condition." Jovie and Jerry gave her their condolences, mentioning of course people they knew who had thyroid conditions like that was going to make a difference. Lexi couldn't help but blatantly roll her eyes at their pointless conversational comments.

"Ah knew this day was comin' soon, thank you fur contactin' me again," Lexi breathed out.

"I'm assuming you saw the signs too?" Jerry inquired.

"Ah knew he was goin' off th' deep end after he told me one evening 'at he bet my stomach would make a fine cookin' pouch fur haggis," she casually said while staring down at her roly-poly belly.

Jovie and Jerry both gave each other a glance that said, *Did I hear that correctly?* Unfortunately, the telekinesis glance was confirmation, that they indeed, did hear that correctly.

"That's disturbing," Jovie commented.

"Quite," Lexi agreed. That was the end of that awkward interaction as Lexi turned around and began waddling away. The way she walked reminded Jovie of a goose, her ass swishing back and forth, with her one pigeon-toed foot curved inward.

"Sure hope Sherpa never face plants into that," Jerry uttered.

"You and me both" Jovie admitted.

"I heard my naaaaaame!" Sherpa yelled from behind them.

I swear that little girl has super hearing or something, Jerry thought to himself. Even if you whispered her name in the house, she somehow always heard it and would come over questioning you like some damn cute little detective. If you played dumb to her questions she would give you that look like she knew you were full of shit.

Sherpa jumped out in front of them with her Tinker Bell costume on from last Halloween.

"You can call me Tink!" she announced proudly with her hands on her hips, looking off majestically to the right. Sanjay poked his head out from around his parents to look at his little sister's masquerade.

"Hi, Stink" he said so matter of fact, waving his hand in front of his nose. Both Jovie and Jerry couldn't help but crack a smile while Sherpa's face suddenly changed once she realized what he had called her.

"Hey! I'm not dinky! You're dinky, Sanjay!" she yelled defensively while stomping a foot down and crossing her arms. Jerry and Jovie giggled to themselves as they heard her still mumbling to herself, "You dink, Sanjay, You dink. I don't dink, you dink."

It was dinnertime for the Wintuks as they all sat down. Jerry had prepared dinner this night. He and Jovie usually switched off depending on one another's schedule and mood. He was an excellent cook, and quite enjoyed it as well. Tonight's menu included a whole roasted chicken flavored with lemon and sage, steamed vegetables flavored with rosemary, and a baby green salad tossed in a balsamic dressing with almonds, feta cheese, and dried blueberries.

"Bon appetit!" he yelled as he set down the last dish in the middle of the table. The family dug in as their mouths watered from the delicious smells and sight. Jovie noticed Sierra's eyes were bothering her as she kept rubbing them.

"Sierra, what's wrong with your eyes, hunny?"

"They've been irritated ever since Tinker Bell over here blew glitter into them," she answered while pointing over at Sherpa. Everyone at the table looked over at little Sherpa at the same time with judging eyes.

"I'm sorry," she said while looking down, you could hear her voice cracking.

"You don't need to cry about it," Sierra said with a retort in her tone.

"I'll never do dat again, Sierra," Sherpa said, becoming very emotional. The age of a toddler was such a delicate time in one's life, everything was so emotional as you were bombarded with different and new feelings constantly. Right now for Sherpa, the emotion she was experiencing was guilt and remorse, with a touch of embarrassment.

All the Wintuks stopped eating and looked at one another in awe, Sierra looked at her sister, "What did you say?"

Sherpa began crying harder now, "I said, I'll never do dat again, Sierra."

Sierra jumped up from her chair to give Sherpa the biggest hug ever, while Jovie, Jerry, and Sanjay all began clapping. Sherpa was confused as she wiped away tears and stared at them with her big blinking eyes that always appeared too large for her face.

Sierra grabbed her sister's face, pushing her hair out of the way and said, "You did it, Sherpa! You did it!" Sherpa was still obviously confused and looked at all of them, trying to figure it out. "You said, Sierra! You didn't call me Sara!" Sherpa's face lit up as her confidence was restored and her happiness rebooted from the inside out.

"Sierra! Sierra! I did it!" Sherpa shrieked back, as she clapped her hands together and gazed over, scanning all of her family member's faces as they smiled at her and cheered her on. Sherpa felt like

she was on cloud nine at that moment as her
emotions did a complete one-eighty, feeling loved
and proud now.

<h1 style="text-align:center">Chapter Twelve</h1>

Sanjay stared at himself in the mirror as he buttoned up his freshly ironed white shirt and folded his collar. It was the first day of sex education class, and he was excited to say the least. Previously he had already taken a class similar to this but now that he was older, he had high hopes for this one and was eager to learn about the mysterious sensual wonders of the female body. He snuck into his parent's bathroom, spraying his dad's finest cologne on himself and putting his mom's lotion on his dry scaly hands. Running downstairs he yelled his goodbyes to his parents, slipping out the front door to meet up with Sierra who was patiently waiting.

Once they reached the school, Sierra went off to her locker while Sanjay met up with his group of friends.

"Jesus, what's that smell, Sanjay?" one of them asked while plugging their nose.

Another boy chimed in, "Its pussy juice to attract the ladies, right Sanjay?"

"Shut up, it's just my deodorant," Sanjay lied through his teeth. "My mom bought a different brand or something. So, it smells different," he said defensively.

The morning bell rang. Sanjay's heart felt like it skipped a few beats as his mind began imagining how the first day of this class would go. Mrs. Mitz was the instructor, and you bet Sanjay and every boy in his class had the hots for her. She was probably in her early thirties, with red flowing hair, creamy pale skin, and big breasts paired with a curvy voluptuous body. She was the definition of 'sexy' in Sanjay's mind. She sort of reminded him of the redhead from a movie his parent's made him watch once, *something about a Roger Rabbit*. He couldn't remember now. Of course she never could wear anything low cut at this Catholic school, but she did wear these cute cardigans that would button up in the center. The buttons always appeared like they were just about to pop off and her breasts would come bursting out like an unwrapped present.

She's so beautiful, Sanjay thought as he stared at her.

"I thought we would start off with some music for the first day. I'm going to pass out the lyrics to this song, then I want everyone to read along to themselves silently while I play the song," she explained. She passed out the printed lyrics to the class saying, "Now, I don't expect any of you to know this song. I bet your parents would know it. It's called *'Tempted'* by a group called Squeeze. Here we go," she said as the song began to play. The song played out, some kids giggled at parts of the song, while others seemed to be enjoying it. Sanjay just sat there thinking about Mrs. Mitz though, and how gorgeous she was. "So, what did you all think?" she asked while leaning against her desk. Not one person in the class raised their hand, she began scanning the room.

Dammit, Sanjay thought to himself. He hated when teachers would do that, they would just scan the room for a victim, back and forth…back and forth…gaging…gaging…

"Sanjay!" she exclaimed. Now, what Sanjay meant to say next was, "Mrs. Mitz," however as he stared at her, all that escaped his horny mouth was, "Mrs. Tits."

The class fell silent, then an enormous rupture of laughter echoed throughout the classroom.

She stared at Sanjay, now crossing her arms, "Excuse me?" she asked while lowering her glasses. Sanjay could feel himself blushing and his body temperature increase as beads of sweat developed on his forehead.

"Mrs. Mitz! Sorry, Mrs. Mitz!" he said genuinely and with embarrassment.

Fuck!

"Anyways, the chorus of this song repeatedly says, 'tempted by the fruit of another,' does anyone care to elaborate on that?" The class switched gears now and the focus was the song, everyone putting in their two cents and collaborating. After the discussion dwindled, Mrs. Mitz went on to say something along the lines of, "…And this is why we wait until after marriage to have sex and give in to our temptations for the fruit of another only after then. Now take the Garden of Eden as an example…" Sanjay had stopped listening again at this point, still thinking about his embarrassing moment and how stupid he felt. Oh, how the class was going to forever remember this moment and all eyes would always be on Sanjay, judging him until the day he died. Not really, or even realistically, but that's how Sanjay felt and every kid his age whenever they did something stupid or embarrassing.

You think the kid Davie over there, back of the class to the left, is going to look back thirty years from now and say, "Remember the time that Indian kid said Mrs. Tits instead of Mrs. Mitz?" No. Well, it's not impossible but it's highly unlikely. Even if, that's one kid out of a class of at least twenty-five kids. Kids around Sanjay's age never thought that way though, not until a few years later down the line. Then, there were always those few who never made it out of that state of mind. Those were the kids who would later become self-absorbed adults, thinking the world revolved around them all the time, not even realizing how insignificant they were in the world. Ignorance is bliss.

Chapter Thirteen

"Psssst, psssst. Aye Tink, Tinkerbell. It's mae, Angus," *he* whispered in the night. Sherpa groggily woke up, rubbing her eyes. She insisted on wearing her costume to bed every night, only removing the wings before sleep and putting them back on when she awoke. She walked over to her open bedroom window to find Angus staring at her, it appeared he had already removed the screen. She reached down and pinched herself,

"Not dreamin' Tink, this is real. I'm sorry if yer dreams of mae before were a tad scary, I'm a good bloke," *he* assured her.

Sherpa thought about this, then responded, "Den why did you kill dat poor butterfly? I saw you do it out da window."

"Oh! That? Actually, ah was doin' a good thing!" *he* lied through his dentures. "See, 'at butterfly was about to kill a fairy, but th' fairy was too wee fur you to see. Butterflies are fairies enemies, ye didn't know that?" *he* said convincingly. She shook her head, indicating she wasn't aware of this knowledge.

"What are you doing here, Anus?" she whispered in her petite voice. He made a disgruntled face at this mispronunciation on her part but ignored it.

"Do ye want tae be a fairy, Sherpa? Ye can be Tink fur real, not just pretend," *he* pointed out luringly. She looked at *him*, her eyes beginning to water with excitement, "Ye do, don't ye?" *he* asked with validation.

"More dan anyding," she confirmed with a smile and glistening eyes.

"Come wit mae then, Tink!" *he* whispered with excitement and promise. *He* began drooling as *his* dentures popped out with eagerness, quickly pushing them back in and smiling.

"Can you put my wings on for me, Anus?" she asked quietly.

"Only if ye can promise mae something," *he* looked at her sternly now as she gazed up at *him*, nodding her head in agreement. "Ye got tae start callin' me somethin' else…please. An' when we get to the magical fairy kingdom, ah mae look a wee bit different, maybe scary, but I'm th' same Angus, ok? Promise mae ye won't be scared?" *he* asked.

"Can I call you, pirate?" she asked.

"Sure Tink, that'll do. Better than th' alternative," he responded.

"I promise, pinky promise. I won't be scared, pirate," she comforted *him* while holding her pinky out.

Sherpa handed *him* her fairy wings as *he* attached them to her costume in the back. The two of them snuck out her bedroom window and made their way to *his* car—a Subaru Outback, of course. It was a much older model but still one nonetheless. Sherpa noticed *he* didn't have *his* cane with *him* and seemed to be moving better than usual, *his* balance and movement seemed to be up to par. The moon was full that night and appeared to take up the whole sky, brimming with brilliance and luminosity. The air smelled sweet and fireflies danced around Sherpa's head.

What little Sherpa didn't realize was, fireflies were pretty uncommon in the state of California. The closest thing you got to guaranteed fireflies in this state was at Disneyland on the Pirates of the

Caribbean ride. At the beginning of the attraction, when the old man is rocking in his chair at night by a bayou while you slowly drifted by.

Angus buckled her up in the backseat and pressed play on his tape cassette as they began their adventure. *'Moonlight Serenade'* by Glenn Miller filled the noise in the car as they bounced around very cartoon-like up the winding road leading to the redwoods. Sherpa was too distracted by the playful fireflies and whimsical music that she didn't seem to notice the physical changes taking place within Angus. As they made their way up the twisting road, *his* facial features began transforming. Higher and higher now up the mountain, *his* hat that once laid atop *his* head, was being pushed off by mushrooming horns.

"Um, are you ok, pirate?" Sherpa asked with concern in her voice.

"Remember what I said? Some changes are going to happen, everything is ok," *he* assured her.

"You sound different," she blurted.

"Well, yes, the closer we get to the woods— magical fairy kingdom, the more I change," *he* said to her, no ounce of a Scottish accent was left in *his* voice. *His* voice was now much deeper and vigorous sounding. She noticed *his* hands appeared more claw-like, with long fingers and black nails extending as *he* swished a finger back and forth to the music, humming along. "You excited about becoming a fairy, Tink?" *he* asked her in order to ease any tension.

She lit up again, "Mhmm! I can't wait!" she responded.

"Me neither," he replied as an unnerving smile escalated across his face.

Jovie and Jerry were downstairs conducting their usual morning routine. It was Mother's Day. A bouquet of flowers sat on the table in a vase, "Happy Mother's Day, Jove," Jerry said to her. She leaned in, giving him a smooch and a hug.

"I wonder what the kids made me," she said.

"They showed me yesterday," he responded.

"Oh yea?" she said as her face beamed, her Wisconsinian roots really coming out whenever she said that phrase. Sierra could be heard running down the stairs and jumping to skip the last step as usual.

Though, this time, instead of Sierra poking her head in and saying, "Sherpa is still sleeping" like she usually did, she ran in asking, "Sherpa in here?"

Jovie and Jerry both stopped what they were doing and gave Sierra the same look, the look said, *What?*

Sierra panicked now, clarifying, "Sherpa! She's not in her bed! Her window is wide open and the screen is gone!" The three of them went running upstairs to her room, Sanjay was already at the scene. Jovie began shaking, falling to the floor from weakness in her legs.

Jerry bent down and held Jovie, "Jove, we're gonna figure this out, ok? But, we need to stay strong in the meantime. We're no good to anyone or even each other if we don't stay strong," he said to her in a shaking scared shitless voice.

"You guys, look," Sanjay said while pointing towards the open window.

"It's an animabus damnatis," Sierra said. They all stared at the half-naked male, this one had a deer's head on, with large antlers.

"What?" Jerry asked.

"That's what they're called, *he* told me one of the times *he* visited. *He* said we keep calling them 'horned things.' Then, corrected me and said they're called animabus damnatises," Sanjay answered.

"*He* visited me when I passed out at the talent show," Sierra added. Before Jerry and Jovie could inquire more on this matter, the animabus damnatis waved, Sierra then raised her hand, slowly waving back. He began running away, then landing onto all four limbs, hopping over the backyard fence.

"Why do I feel like we need to follow him?" Sanjay said while looking out the window. The animabus damnatis stopped and turned around now, staring at them, walking a few steps, and then looking back again.

"Because we do, he wants us to follow him. Dad—dad, he's waiting for us to follow him. I think he may be trying to help," Sierra pointed out.

"Shit, we need a car, Jer. Why don't we still have a damn car!" Jovie screamed out now in frustration and panic.

"Because Jove! We were waiting for something other than a Subaru Outback to become available! Remember!" Jerry screamed back.

"Focus!" Sierra and Sanjay both yelled at their parents.

———————

They all ran to Angus's front door, ringing the doorbell repeatedly.

"Oh, come on! Open the door old man!" Jerry yelled.

"Lexi! Lexi!" Jovie yelled, hopeful she would be there.

"Angus's Subaru isn't here Jove, Lexi must be out. If anything, we need to take the other car in the garage," he said.

Jerry ran to the backyard to see if the slider was unlocked, *Aha!* He swiftly slid it open. He sprinted into the dark stuffy house, that still somehow always had smoke swirling around in its stagnant air. "Hello! Hello!" Jerry yelled as he frantically searched for any sign of car keys.

The house smelled of someone cooking or at least had recently been cooking. *Must have just missed them*, Jerry thought to himself. He made his way through the dining room…stopping dead in his tracks as he froze in disbelief. He could feel himself becoming ill as he was trying to make sense of what he was staring at. It was Lexi. She was completely naked, laying on the dining table, belly up. Her stomach appeared to already have been removed, stuffed and cooked, and placed back in…it was sliced down the middle, with what looked like haggis pouring out. Jerry became violently ill, vomiting as he grabbed onto a chair, trying to steady himself. He regained control, wiping vomit from his chin and clenching his stomach as he continued to search for the car keys. He found a key holder by the front door, with hooks at the bottom that held dangling keys.

He saw them glisten in the dimly lit house, grabbing them and yelling through the front door, "I

found the keys! I'll meet you outside the garage!"
He didn't want his family to have to endure what he
just did.

He pressed the button to open the garage, getting
in to start the car as his family all followed. To
Jerry's surprise, the car started up no problem.
Urgently putting the car in reverse, the Wintuks
squealed out of the driveway.

"Where is he?" Jerry asked as they all peered out
the windows, scanning the suburban neighborhood
for any movement.

"There!" Jovie yelled, "I saw something moving
around over there, in those hydrangeas." The family
studied the flowering bush as it rustled back and
forth, finally seeing antlers popping out. Jovie
raised her fingers to her mouth and blew out a
whistle, this made the animabus damnatis poke his
head up, standing up now on two feet. He began
running as they followed closely behind, you could
tell he was making sure not to run too fast as he
didn't want to lose them. To not run too quickly, he
never dropped on all fours, just kept running with
his two legs only.

He's taking us to our old house, Jovie thought to
herself as she started to realize where he was
leading them to. She didn't know how, but this
thing—animabus damnatis, didn't seem phased or
tired by all the running it had and still was currently
doing. They made a few more turns until they took
the one road that twisted and turned up the
mountain into the redwoods.

"Why is he taking us here?" Jerry asked aloud,
partially to himself but also for his family to hear.

"He's taking us to the beginning," Jovie
answered without hesitation. "This all started

happening when we lived here, in the redwoods," Jovie continued.

"I thought the whole point of us having that house destroyed was so none of this would happen, and now it's happening. *He* followed us out of the woods," Sierra said with defeat.

Sanjay could see something moving from the corner of his eye, "Look!" he yelled. One by one, more and more animabus damnatises appeared from the surrounding forest, both male and female, some had deer heads while others had ram and goat heads. It was a stampede of them now running, not only in front of the vehicle, but also behind it, and on the sides.

"What the—?" Jerry murmured as he looked around.

"It's almost as if they're helping us? Or protecting us in some way?" Jovie expressed.

Then, a flock of half-human, half bat-looking creatures swooped down, hitting the windshield of the car. They all screamed as the hair rose on the back of their necks and cracks dispersed across the windshield. It appeared the flying creatures and the pack of animabus damnatises were beginning a war. The Wintuks watched as this demoniac brutal apocalyptic scene played out in front of them. One flying creature picked an animabus damnatis up by its antlers and swung it with mighty force against a tree, killing it instantly. Then, another flying creature that had made a landing was immediately attacked by a gang of animabus damnatises, all charging with heads down and horns out. The whole free-for-all was one gigantic blood-splattered hodgepodge.

It all happened so fast, and like that, the gory scene was over as the herd of animabus damnatises kept running along, making sure the Wintuks were still safely following.

"What the hell just happened?" Jovie said aloud.

"I think a part of Hell just happened," Jerry said, still in a state of shock and confusion. The four of them all sat in their own ozone of stupor as *'Moonlight Serenade'* by Glenn Miller began to play on the radio.

"I thought we couldn't get any radio stations up here," Sanjay said with a stone-cold face.

"We can't" Jerry answered, reaching over to turn it off as it was making him uncomfortable with unknowingness. The radio wouldn't turn off, none of the buttons did anything, not even the volume dial was doing anything. They sat in silence as they continued up the mountain where it would still be at least another half an hour drive to the beginning of *him.*

Chapter Fourteen

Sherpa and who she still believed to be Angus, walked through the redwoods now, holding hands and both smiling.

"Ahh, nothing like the fresh air here," *he* said while breathing in deeply through *his* bat snout, then exhaling loudly.

Sherpa decided to imitate *him*, breathing in deeply and exhaling as loud as her little body could, "Ahhh," she agreed. "Pirate?" she asked inquisitively.

"Yes, Tink?" *he* acknowledged.

"You sord of remind me of dis ding my family and I saw in the woods before. It was bad," she pointed out.

"Oh yes, there's a lot of us in these woods, some bad and some good. That must have been a bad one, I'm a good one. I'm still Angus—or to you, pirate. Just look different when I'm here, but change back when I'm down the mountain," *he* explained.

"Is dat what it will be like when you turn me into a fairy? I be a fairy in the woods, but den when I'm out, I'm normal Sherpa again? Cause, I still want to live with my mama and papa, and broder and sister," she expressed.

"Of course Sherpa! Of course! You'll have the best of both worlds, just like me," *he* implied optimistically. She smiled at this and nodded her head, breathing in the woodsy air again.

"I'll be Tink here—and Sherpa there!" she exclaimed.

"Exactly!" *he* concurred enthusiastically.

"You know what else smells really good?" *he* asked.

"What?" she responded.

"Lily of the valley flowers. You ever smelled one? It smells so sweet, like candy!" *he* said. Studying her, *he* could tell by her expression she was becoming uncomfortable.

"What is it, Tink?" *he* asked with lying concern.

"I promised my sister I wouldn't have anyding to do with dat," she said while looking down.

"But was it a pinky promise?" *he* asked.

"Yes," she answered. *He* actually wasn't expecting that answer from her.

"But what about our pinky promise?" *he* whined. *He* grabbed a bouquet of the white flowers, holding them up and saying, "They're good, see, the fairies live inside of these flowers, it's their home." *He* sniffed in a whiff, "Ah, home sweet home, Tink. Home sweet home." She stared down again, thinking about this, then gazing back up at the flowers *he* was grasping.

"I don't see any fairies living in der," she said while analyzing *him*.

"Well, that's because you aren't a fairy yet! I can see them because I already have magical powers to do so. Once you're a fairy, you can see them too!" *he* assured her.

He could see her hesitation and sense her worry, *its time to wine and dine her so to speak, he* thought to himself. *Butter her up. He* pointed his tapering claw-like finger towards a spot in the woods, radiance shone down like a stage light through the towering trees, illuminating particles in the crisp air. A large portobello mushroom erupted through the earth, and two toadstools on either end, serving as chairs. Lily of the valley flowers began bursting up and out, massive now as if Sherpa either shrunk or they grew at least a hundred times their normal size. The dangling white flowers that resembled bells lit up now as the forest around them grew dim. Fireflies fluttered around, entering the inside of the bell-like flowers as if they were light bulbs for these flower-shaped shades.

Sherpa admired the transformation around her taking place as she stood there in complete fixation. *He* sat down on the larger of the toadstools, motioning for her to come and sit across from *him* on the other. She skipped over to *him* and sat across, putting her elbows on the makeshift portobello table, hands framing her chin.

"Time for a tea party, Tink," *he* said. She clapped her hands with eagerness and excitement at this idea. A swarm of fireflies carried a teapot and cups over to them, but what Sherpa didn't know was, the 'tea' was a concoction made up of lily of the valley flowers. *He* poured her a cup, offering sugar cubes, which then of course she agreed to. She stirred the sugar cubes into her tea, feeling surreal and lucky at the same time that this was happening to her. She continued to sip her warm tea and soak in the magnificently magical ambiance that surrounded her.

The tea's side effects began kicking in as Sherpa started to feel nauseous and somewhat disoriented.

"I feel sick," she mumbled, cupping her hand over her small tummy.

"Oh, that's normal, you have to drink the full cup if you want to be a fairy," *he* encouraged her. She grabbed the teacup with both hands now, lifting it to her lips and drinking it down. Sherpa wanted so badly to be a fairy, even if that meant getting sick to her stomach. She glanced around the forest, her vision becoming blurrier and blurrier as her mouth began to salivate uncontrollably. She became not only weak but extremely confused and vulnerable as her symptoms were worsening. The forest started to change around them, the larger than life bell-like flowers shrunk back down to a regular size. The once perfect and enchanted looking mushroom table and chair set were now a soggy and smelly mess, with squirming maggots covering it. The fireflies were now June beetles, flying into Sherpa's face and body annoyingly due to poor eyesight. Groggily, she attempted to wave them away with her petite hands, failing miserably. The redwoods around her began doing what she remembered once before—bleeding. Blood crept out from the crevices that grooved between the bark, down the tall trees, and onto the dirt. Again, like previously, wherever the blood was flowing, lily of the valley flowers were breaking through the dirt and rising.

The forest floor began to shake as the miniature streams of blood pooled together in the center. The sound of large roots being broken and snapped could be heard throughout the forest as something was being pushed up from the earth below. Then, an enormous monumental staircase came spiraling out like a corkscrew. The whole staircase appeared to look like an antique, with its wooden steps that appeared somewhat dusty or dirty from the earth; you couldn't tell which. The wooden steps had a slight reddish hue to them which pointed all fingers to redwood. The rest was pretty simple, with tall tarnished iron rods and a matching railing to go with it. The decorative piece at the beginning of the staircase, right before the railing formed was a unique one, it was a pair of antlers.

Sherpa felt too sick and disoriented to speak or even think logically at this point.

"You must walk up those stairs, Tin-**k**," *he* said to her, enunciating the 'k' syllable out of fun and arrogance. Since she was too ill to speak, she gave him a desperate stare. "If you just walk up to the top of the stairs, and jump off, I promise you, your pain will end and you'll finally get to be a fairy. Pinky promise," *he* said while holding *his* pinky out to her.

The Wintuks finally made it to the desired location—or what they assumed was since they were just following the pack of animabus damnatises. It was an empty dirt lot, surrounded by a circle of redwoods, where they're lovely house once stood before they had it destroyed. The radio, which they all were damn aware they had zero control over, started playing '*This Must Be The Place,*' by *The Talking Heads*. The four of them glanced at one another, in wonderment and suspicion. Angus's other vehicle that *he* drove, was sitting there, abandoned. Suddenly, that car radio turned on as well, playing the same song as both car radios volume began turning up more and more. The Wintuks all jumped out of the car as the music was blaring into the tunnels of their ears like a vortex that broke all laws of physics.

Jovie mumbled to herself, "This is the place."

All of the animabus damnatises dispersed, running in all directions of the forest, except for one, it was the one that led them there, to begin with. He stared at them from a distance, as they stared back, waiting for a queue of some sort. He waved, Sierra waved back as she did before.

"Well, let's follow him," she said to the rest of her family as she took the first step in his direction. Following the animabus damnatis into the forest, within a single line formation, they glanced around at the scenery they once had the privilege of admiring before on a daily basis. He stopped, turning around to look at them and raised a finger to where his mouth would be if he didn't have the animal head on, signaling for them to stay quiet. The Wintuks all nodded at him, signaling that they understood and would obey his direction.

Then, *he* could be heard nearby.

"You're doing great, Tink. Keep going and your wings will become real," is what they picked up as they eavesdropped from behind some trees. Sherpa was moving up the spiral staircase, extremely slow due to the state she was in, almost half crawling and attempting to pull herself up at the same time. She reminded Sierra of a struggling injured animal—or insect because of her fairy wings, that was just using the last of its energy to spend its final moments alone. Sierra so badly wanted to cry out and sprint towards her sister but bit her tongue instead.

What happened next…was the last thing any of the Wintuks imagined, not like this wasn't crazy enough. The animabus damnatis threw a rock in the opposite direction to get *his* attention. It worked, as *he* made a dramatically unpleasant face showing concern and disappointment all at once like a parent would after a teen arrived home after curfew. He grunted deeply as he turned to investigate the disruptive disturbance. The animabus damnatis charged as fast as he could, landing on all fours, and darting up the staircase, pushing Sherpa out of the way like an inpatient canine.

As he approached the top of the stairs, *he* yelled "No!", as *he* turned around and saw what the commotion was. The animabus damnatis jumped from the top, falling to the forest floor to his death. Once he died, his complete human form took shape, no longer was his face disguised by the head of a horned animal.

He picked up the body with his obsidian resembling claw-like nails and threw it with anger across the way, making it land right in front of Jovie. She stared down into the dead eyes looking up at her. The eyes and face she was looking down at, were that of her father's. She covered her mouth and screamed, then ran out of a combination of fear and maternal instincts towards Sherpa. The spiral staircase was now swirling back down into the earth below as it corkscrewed in reverse, leaving Sherpa behind, thankfully. Jovie and the rest of the Wintuks gathered around Sherpa as *he* became irate. *He* pounded *his* beastly fists down as *he* made the forest floors ripple for miles, causing redwoods to rise and fall as roots came snapping out, flinging dirt all around.

"Do you know what that maggot has just done! He ruined everything!" *he* screamed as *his* broad muscular chest puffed up and down as *he* breathed heavily. Jovie had no idea what *he* was referring to exactly, but what she did know, is that was her father's body laying over there, lifeless. She sat there, holding Sherpa in her arms, trying to make sense of it all.

Her father had passed away when she was only seven-years-old, *How is this even possible? How is any of this possible?* "That's my father, Jer," she said to him while nodding her head in the direction of the deceased.

He let out an insane sounding laughter just then, "Oh, that's gold, Jove! Pure gold right there, fucking rich, Jove!" *he* yelled while laughing harder now, *his* eyes tearing up with blood. *He* wiped them away as *his* laughter began to diminish and the corner of *his* mouth gathered a pool of drool again like it was so prone to.

"Your father must have been a pretty bad man to end up with me, Jove," *he* said to her like a snake slithering through its fangs, "to end up with the damnation of souls."

"Where's Angus?" Sanjay asked with confused shifty eyes.

"Angus!" *he* asked with surprise and excitement, "that fuck face is stuck with me! He lives inside of me Sanjay, forever, as long as I need him to. You know he's the only reason I was able to leave the redwoods, and continue terrorizing you and your family?" The whole family gulped and listened with wide eyes and open mouths as *he* continued. "That miserable old man was wondering around, completely unaware of what he was doing. Cops had to pick him up after reports of an old disoriented man. Then the cops were called to these redwoods to help a pathetic family lost in the woods—you're the pathetic family, in case you couldn't figure that one out. Angus sat in the back of one of the cop cars, confused and lost as he stared out the window at you all being wrapped in blankets and taken care of. But poor Angus sat there like an abandoned puppy, just desperate for an owner. Well, I became that weak man's owner. Voila! His sorry lonely soul let me in like a one night stand," *he* grumbled.

This was all sort of coming together now, the pieces of information were now falling into place like a cold case on its way to being solved.

Damnation of souls…damnation of souls…that must be what the animabus damnatises are, Jovie thought to herself. *My father was part of the damned*, she thought again. *He saved Sherpa by intervening with whatever was going on,* Jovie wasn't sure what that was, *a ritual maybe? He sacrificed himself to save Sherpa?* Jovie went back and forth through her thoughts trying to make sense of it all. Jerry on the other hand was bouncing around the realization that Angus had been possessed by *him*—this demon, ever since they left this hell hole, literally.

I didn't like the old man, but he didn't deserve that, Jerry thought to himself.

"Bleh!" little Sherpa began vomiting. Jerry and Jovie both gave each other a look that said, *we need to get her out of here.* Her poor tiny body was shaking and her face was a sickly pale, she wiped the vomit from her mouth, looking up at her parents with teary eyes.

"Am I a fairy yet?" she asked.

Chapter Fifteen

A week had gone by since the day Sherpa almost died at the hands of *him.* The last thing any of the Wintuks remembered, was being gathered around Sherpa, and within a blink of an eye, they were back at home in their living room. None of them could explain how they ended up back at home, but there they were, sitting on the Persian rug that laid in the middle of the room.

Sierra had noticed Sherpa reach down and pinch her thigh, smiling and saying to herself, "Oh, I was just dweaming," as the rest of them glanced at one another giving telekinesis stares that meant, *no one say a thing to her about the whole thing actually not being a dream.*

It was in the middle of the night and neither Sanjay nor Sierra could sleep. They crept out of their bedrooms to eavesdrop on their parents having 'adult talk' in the kitchen. The two of them sat in the dark, halfway down the stairs, listening. Hands fisted under their chins while ears perked wide open, concentrating on the words they were speaking.

Jovie could be heard saying, "Jer, we need to make a move."

Jerry responding with, "What, Jove? We just gonna keep running from this thing?

Huh?" They could hear their mom scoff and ask, "Well what do you propose then Jer?" Sanjay and Sierra looked at each other as silence fell. Staring at one another, anticipating one of them to speak again, for all they could hear was their own hearts beating for fear of the unknown.

"Here," Jovie said as Sierra and Sanjay let out a sigh of relief.

"You want to move there?" Jerry could be heard asking her.

"It's the farthest place from here that's still in the U.S., so yea Jer, I want to move there. I want to be as far away from this place as possible. I don't want to be near any redwood forests or redwoods for that matter," her voice beginning to crack now. You could tell at that moment, Jerry reached out and began hugging his wife. The two siblings didn't have to see it to know that's what was happening, they could sense their parent's affection in the air.

Not only did Sierra and Sanjay share the sense of sibling telekinesis through emotions and stares, but the two of them practiced sign language. Both were enrolled in a sign language course at school and quickly adapted to using it as a means of secretive communication.

"Where do you think we are moving to?" Sierra signed to Sanjay.

"I don't know, Hawaii I hope," Sanjay signed back.

Sierra rolled her eyes and signed to him, "That's not that far, they can't be talking about Hawaii."

"Yea, but it's on an island," he signed back to her.

"What? Sometimes I think you're stupid," she signed to him. He responded with a disgruntled face at this comment, wrinkling his nose in dismay.

"Want to go down to the wine cellar?" Sanjay signed.

"Why? So mom and dad can get mad at us?" Sierra signed.

"They can't hear us down there. We can actually talk. Also, I want to use the chalkboard," he signed.

"Fine," she signed back, rolling her eyes.

The two of them crept as quietly as possible, they knew their mom had owl ears. It seemed as though this was going to be easier than suspected since now their parent's bickering had turned louder and sour.

"Made it," Sanjay breathed out, wiping nonexistent sweat from his forehead as they reached the last step leading down to the cellar. The wine cellar was Sierra and Sanjay's backup safe spot when the fort in the tree trunk wasn't an option. One entire wall was a chalkboard that consisted of random to-do lists, doodles, and two columns, one titled Jovie and the other titled Jerry. They would write down the date and what bottle they opened, then write what they thought about it, along with star ratings. Jovie's column consisted of descriptions such as;

-*velvety with a hint of smoke* ***
-*jammy with underlying tannins* ****
-*fruity and tart* **

While Jerry's descriptions said things like;

-*tastes like wine* *****
-*might have grapes in it* ***
-*is this safe to drink?* *

Sanjay grabbed the chalkboard eraser, clearing the doodles so that they could use the spot for something more important.

"What are you doing?" Sierra asked.

"Let's make a list of what we need when we move," he answered.

"What do you mean? Like boxes?" she asked.

"No, like snow boots, or raincoats, umbrellas, stuff like that. We're moving somewhere completely different, aren't you excited? We don't even own an umbrella, Sierra. Now that I think about it, I don't think either one of us even owns a raincoat," he pointed out. Sierra decided to join in on this 'LiSt of StUff' activity, writing her name and underlining it, then adding underneath it— ScArF.

"Oh, good one. That might make my neck scratchy, hmm…I'll add beanie," Sanjay said. The two of them kept going back and forth, adding things from clothing items to things like sleds and ice skates.

"I'll get us one!" they heard their dad holler out, as his footsteps creaked above them.

"Sanjay!" Sierra whispered, with a worried face that said, *I told you so!* Sanjay ran over to the light switch, turning it off with quick grace and motioned to his sister to hide. Sierra hid behind some barrels while Sanjay hid across from her behind a short stocky fridge that held a collection of cheeses. They could hear their dad walk down the still fresh redwood steps to the cellar, flicking on the main light when he got to the bottom. Sanjay and Sierra both stared at each other, wide-eyed and frightened to be found. Jerry was mumbling to himself as he read the backs of a few different bottles, trying to decipher which one fit his mood. Once a selection was made, he uncorked it, pouring it into a clean glass and swirled it around, sniffing it and then taking a sip. He swished it around in his mouth, then held it on his tongue as he thought about it, ending with a gulp. Jerry walked over to the chalkboard.

"Shit! The chalkboard," Sierra signed to Sanjay.

"Aw, shit," Sanjay signed back, ultimately agreeing with his sister. Both of their hearts raced as they watched their dad, waiting to see if he would notice their new chalkboard addition. Thankfully, he didn't notice their 'LiSt of StUff' and instead added a new wine description under his column;
-makes me feel good *****
He flicked the main light off, making his way back up the stairs. Once the door closed, both Sanjay and Sierra let out a sigh of relief.

"I thought we were done," Sierra said into the darkness to Sanjay.

"Me too," he responded. It was pitch black in the cellar, you couldn't see your own hand in front of your face. Couldn't even sense it if you wanted to, all senses felt blind and disabled at this moment. Sierra began to cry, whimpering now.

"Sierra? What's wrong?" Sanjay asked.

"I don't know, I just—I just—am really scared. I can't see anything," she said.

"I know, it's ok. I'm going to go turn on the switch right now, ok?" he comforted her.

"Can you at least open the fridge for light until you flip the switch?" she asked.

"Yea, good idea," he said back. He reached over to grab the fridge handle—his heart felt as though it stopped beating right in his chest. Like it was frozen solid in his chest cavity.

"What? What is it?" she whined from the darkness. Sanjay was still trying to figure that out, someone else was already holding the fridge handle. He jerked away and ran over to where he believed the light switch to be. He flicked on the lights and what they saw would forever scar them.

It was Angus, crawling on the floor like an insane person, wearing only an adult diaper. He smiled up at the both of them, showing off his rotting teeth. They so badly wanted to scream but were incapable. Disabled, like their senses. He scurried off like a rabid rat behind a stack of barrels.

"I feel like I can't speak. Like I'm incapable," Sierra signed to Sanjay.

"Me too," he signed back. He walked over to the barrels, peering behind them.

"He's not here," Sanjay signed.

"What do you mean, he's not there?" Sierra signed back.

"No one is here," Sanjay signed. The two of them stared at one another as they tried to digest this fact, eyes watering uncontrollably. They crept back upstairs to their bedrooms, neither one getting even an ounce of sleep that night.

The next morning, Jerry and Jovie had the kids miss school so they could pack up and get out of Oyster Shoals. Apparently, the new town they were moving to was known for oysters and lobsters, however, neither were in the name. Go figure, Oyster Shoals had zero oysters while Porte, Maine had tons. Porte, Maine was going to be the Wintuk's new home, the furthest eastern town in the U.S. To be frank, none of them were excited or looking forward to this move at all, but perhaps with time, they would become more accepting, at least that's what Jovie hoped for. Sierra and Sanjay both began their online research on Porte, once they realized that's where they were moving to.

"Complete opposite of Hawaii, Sanjay," Sierra said to him with attitude as they both stared at the computer screen.

"I never been to da snow before," Sherpa said with eagerness as she poked her head between the two of them. She wiggled and wedged her little body between them as she pushed her way forward to get a closer look.

"Excuse you!" Sierra yelled.

"Be nice to her, Sierra. She just wants to see," Sanjay pointed out.

"Yea, SI-ER-RA," Sherpa replied.

"Smartass," Sierra mumbled.

"Bedder than being a dumbass," Sherpa said proudly as she studied the screen.

"You stole that from dad!" Sierra remarked accusingly.

"Sierra, shut up, it's not like dad made that up," Sanjay said, obviously annoyed by her.

Sherpa stared up at Sierra, raising her tiny chubby finger to her mouth and said, "Shhhh."

Sierra stood up and stomped off out of the bedroom. In that moment of frustration, Sierra remembered her family climbing down the large redwood tree as she stood up there. Staring at the oozing amber transparent sap as it glistened in the sunlight. How sticky her hands were, how normally that would have peeved her beyond just being annoyed, how small and insignificant it was to be…upset. She turned around to sit back down with her brother and sister, smiling at both of them as they studied her face for any sign of emotion.

"Come join us, Sierra!" Sherpa yelled joyfully as she patted the spot next to her. Sanjay and Sierra both smiled at each other, slightly giggling at Sherpa's naive innocence and enthusiasm.

"I've never been to the snow either, Sherpa," Sierra said while putting an arm around her baby sister.

"Me neither," Sanjay chimed in.

"It'll be a first for all three of us living someplace where there are actually seasons. Look at the trees in this picture," Sierra said while pointing at the image on the screen.

"Der so pretty, is like if I mix my red, orange, and yewow play-doh together, like in a ball," Sherpa described while forming an imaginary play-doh ball with her hands. Sanjay and Sierra both glanced over at each other.

"Sure!" Sanjay exclaimed.

"Exactly!" Sierra voiced second.

The Wintuks were on their way to a state where the trees masked themselves into these breathtaking colors. Where the leaves turned into colors of fire—rather than being on fire. The Wintuks would definitely not miss that part of California. They packed bags to bring with them on the drive there, as well as shipped many boxes to the home they arranged to rent. It was all happening so fast, but Jovie and Jerry felt this needed to happen sooner than later for everyone's well-being.

Chapter Sixteen

It'd been about three months since the Wintuks arrived in Porte, and it has been…glorious actually. Gloriously calm, secure, refreshing, and Jovie and Jerry could both agree, a lot more friendly. The people here were much more welcoming than any Californian they'd met. It frightened both of them a little bit at first since they weren't used to it—which is sad really. It threw them off to be perfectly honest. As some more time went on though, they realized people were just a whole lot nicer here, or maybe just in all other states in general, they honestly weren't sure. Not to say all Californians weren't welcoming, but it was hard to find the 'true ones', as Jerry and Jovie referred to them as. When you found those few, you needed to hold onto them. Southern California on the other hand was the hardest place to find any 'true ones', since there was a high population of materialistic make-believes always trying to keep up with the Joneses. Hence, this is why they chose northern California over southern. None of that seemed to matter anymore, now that they were in Porte, Maine, where the people were friendly and life just seemed more simple. Simple living was all they ever wanted.

The home they were renting was a cute quaint one with a victorian twist and decorative stained glass windows strategically placed throughout the house. It was registered as a historical building along with the lighthouse on the property too. The inside of the lighthouse had a spiral staircase that led to the beacon on top, which Sherpa refused to go up, understandably. She told her family she had a nightmare once about a spiral staircase, no surprise there. Sanjay and Sierra enjoyed going up there though, taking turns of looking through the telescope aimed at the sea. Attached to the large beautiful home, was a greenhouse as well with an enormous decorative cast iron frame that housed slates of glass. All four corners of the greenhouse had iron points on top and a glass dome in the center. At the edge of the outdoor entrance was a gargoyle that crouched over where one would walk in. It seemed like your stereotypical haunted house, however, it was far from it. It was the most at home the Wintuks had ever felt and this lovely home was to not fall under stereotypes. For it deserved much more respect than that.

Sanjay and Sierra started their first few weeks a little rough at school, but once the other kids got to know them, it worked out for the both of them. The kids of Porte weren't as welcoming as the adults, but within the coming weeks, they accepted Sanjay and Sierra, calling them now by their actual names instead of Californio and California. That was annoying, but kids, especially teenagers, were really good at that. For once, the kids were at a public school instead of the private Catholic school they were only previously exposed to. Jovie was secretly happy about this, while Jerry just felt sort of indifferent about the whole thing. Sierra finally got to wear her clothes to school, instead of just uniforms. This had a huge positive impact on her, she felt like she could finally be comfortable and herself in her own skin for once. Sanjay was struggling in this area, but it was a work in progress. One morning he walked downstairs wearing striped pants and a plaid shirt, his parents looked at him and both almost had coffee spray out of their mouths.

While Sherpa had orange juice squirting out of her nose, pointing and yelling "You look ridiculous, Sanjay!" Of course, after his bruised ego, he slumped back upstairs and changed into an outfit that was more…fitting. If your four-year-old sister even knows you look ridiculous, then you've got some work to do in that department.

Sherpa was getting up earlier these days, not just to witness Sanjay's fashion sense, but also to feel more mature. She insisted on having her morning orange juice in a mug, not a sippy cup. Or so she thought was pure orange juice; her parents would secretly cut half of it with water. She would raise it to her lips and slurp the juice from the mug, just like her mom did with her coffee.

"Sluuuurp, ahhh," could be heard from the two of them in unison. She also insisted on reading the morning news in between her mom and dad, except her version of the morning news was *The Very Hungry Caterpillar* book. At least that's what her book of choice was as of lately, by next week it could be something totally different, just like her food choices. She was still going through that age of constant ever-changing phases.

Jovie and Jerry had also gotten back into their old evening routine that consisted of drinking red wine on the front porch while they caught each other up on their days. Some might even say they caught each other up on their now boring days. Boring days were better than what they were experiencing prior, and Jovie and Jerry would tell you, their days aren't boring—they're simple.

Simplicity was the ultimate goal, and as Jerry would say to his wife, "By Jove, I think we've done it!" As they clinked their glasses together. The Wintuks moved to Porte at the beginning of June, and now it was the month of September. Up until now, the weather was nice and comfortable for them in their Californian skins, however, they were in for a more drastic change then they had imagined and this evening would their first taste.

"You can only play outside if you put a jacket on!" Jerry yelled over to the kids.

"I'm going to grab mine, you want yours?" he asked Jovie while looking over at her. She nodded her head and rubbed her shoulders, implying to him that she was indeed cold. The family went outside as Jerry and Jovie sat in their usual spot, gazing at the sun that was to near sunset soon. Sherpa sat in her tiny chair next to them, drinking warm milk out of a mug and inspecting a crossword puzzle in the newspaper. She kept tapping the pencil she was holding to her head like that was going to make her think better, with crinkled eyebrows and her tongue sticking out the corner of her mouth.

"Hmmm," she would say to herself as she scribbled nonsense onto the puzzle, Jerry and Jovie would glance at each other and smile whenever she did this.

The two older kids quickly put their jackets on as they clumsily ran out front, sprinting to the lighthouse and stumbling as they did.

"Kids," Sherpa said while shaking her head, looking back down at her now illegible crossword puzzle.

"You can say that again," Jovie agreed, trying to stay serious as she and Jerry smiled big at one another from the corner of their eyes. Sanjay and Sierra raced each other up the spiral stairs in the lighthouse, both completely out of breath by the time they reached the top.

"Look! It's Mortimer!" Sanjay yelled while pointing out to the sea. Sierra peeked her eye into the telescope, seeing Mortimer on his boat, greeting them with a wave, and a sailor smile. Most people in town called him Mr. Mortimer, but the Wintuks had all sort of resolved to just calling him only Mortimer. He was a very friendly, wacky sort of man who appeared to be somewhere in his seventies, with a long grey beard and a thermos of coffee always in one hand, constantly jacked up on caffeine. As Sierra continued to peek through the scope, she could see him bend down and pick something up.

"He has lobsters!" she yelled in delight.

"Let me see, move!" Sanjay replied impatiently. There was Mortimer, holding them up and lifting the lid from an ice chest to present all his gathered morsels.

"Do you think he's gonna share?" Sierra asked aloud.

"Of course he will, he always shares with us," Sanjay said.

"Because he doesn't have anyone else to share with," Sierra responded. Sanjay thought this was an interesting comment, he never really looked at it that way before, but Sierra's observation made sense and she was probably right. "I'm getting cold," Sierra murmured.

"Me too," Sanjay agreed. With the sun beginning to set and the evening breeze picking up, it was definitely getting chilly and was much chillier at the top of the lighthouse than below. Thankfully, Mortimer had already touched land by this time as the sea grew choppier and more tenacious with the disheveled current.

Sierra and Sanjay scurried down the cement stairs towards the slit of light poking in through the cracked door leading out of the lighthouse.

They could already hear the voice of Sherpa calling out, "Hi, Mort! Mort! Hi, Mort!" There was Mortimer trucking up the grassy hillside to their home, sporting his black fishing boots, overalls, and neon orange beanie. He had a bucket in one hand and his ultra-large thermos in the other, taking swigs from it as he made his way over. Sanjay ran over, taking the bucket from him and carrying it with better grace and balance than Mortimer had been.

"We're eating like kings and queens tonight, kids!" he bragged delightfully, taking another swig of coffee as he pulled his beanie off, exposing a messy gray and white nest of hair.

"Are you eating over, Mortimer?" Sierra questioned.

"Well, your mom and dad, or as your mom would say, 'ma and pa,'"—in his best midwestern accent—"invited me here for dinner, or again as she would say, 'supper,' so yes, I'm eating over miss Sierra," he answered. The three kids all smiled and cheered, for Mortimer was the best neighbor they've ever had, not to mention the closest; in physical terms that is. Jovie and Jerry both greeted Mortimer as they got up from their chairs on the porch, opening the front door for them to all scurry in. You could tell Mortimer was pretty comfortable in the Wintuk's home by now since he knew exactly where the whiskey was and was aware of the unsaid welcome to serve himself. So he did just that, grabbing a short glass and pouring himself a glass of 'medicine,' as he often called it.

"What we got here, Mort?" Jerry asked him. "Lobster of course, and I might have gone oyster hunting beforehand," he said back.

"Oysters!?" Sanjay exclaimed as his mouth began salivating. Sanjay and both his parents loved oysters on the half shell and if given the chance would eat about three dozen each. Sierra and Sherpa on the other hand loathed oysters and often compared them to snot bullets.

"How do you like your oysters, Sanjay?" Mortimer asked.

"Raw of course, on the half shell, with a dab of horseradish, drops of cocktail sauce and tabasco, and lots of squeezed lemon!" he answered without hesitation.

"Mmm, that's the way I like them too," Mortimer agreed, nodding his head while taking a sip of whiskey.

"Gross snot bullets," Sierra mumbled under her breath.

"Yea! Gross snot buwets, dey sort of salty like snot too!" Sherpa announced. Everyone gave her an odd stare stirred with disgust after that comment.

"I'm not even going to ask," Sierra said.

"Wine, eh?" Mortimer inquired while staring at Jerry and Jovie's glasses. "Oh, you Californians and your wine, just wait til' winter hits, then you'll switch to whiskey. It's the only thing that'll warm the soul," he added. "You ever shoveled snow before, Sanjay?" he questioned.

"No, never," he responded.

"Oh, this should be fun," Mortimer commented while chuckling to himself. Sierra couldn't stop staring at the whiskey in the glass, she was almost mesmerized by it, though she didn't know why. She stared as Mortimer raised it to his lips, taking a sip and slamming it back down, watching the caramel-colored whiskey slide down the sides. She realized it reminded her of the amber sap from the redwoods.

"Why don't you take a picture, it'll last longer," Sanjay said smirkingly.

Sierra ignored his comment, "Can I smell that?" she asked Mortimer.

"Sure," he said while sliding the glass across the wooden dining table to her. She took an enormous whiff, expecting it to smell differently than it did.

"Oh, God!" she said while pushing the glass across the table back over to Mortimer as he laughed at her reaction.

"Well, what'd ya think it was going to smell like, miss Sierra?" he inquired.

"For some reason I imagined it to smell like tree sap," she responded softly, almost embarrassed, feeling stupid now.

"Not sap, that's for sure. If you wanna smell tree sap, Sierra, just walk outside towards the woods. There's no shortage of pines in Maine, that's for sure. We have more pines than people!" he said.

"Do you have dose white flowers here, Mort? Dey are called lily of da valley," Sherpa blurted out.

The other four Wintuks all glanced at one another with questioning eyes and telekinetic stares.

Mortimer gave her a funny, sort of puzzled look and said, "Why no, Sherpa. I'm sure they could grow around here, but I don't believe I've ever encountered any," he answered.

Jovie quickly jumped in to change the subject, "How about those oysters and lobsters!" she said while rubbing her hands together in delight. Sierra rolled her eyes as she looked over to see Sanjay already stuffing a napkin into the top of his shirt like a bib.

Jerry had already started heating a large pot of water on the stovetop, which now was at a rolling boil, dropping the lobsters in.

Eeeeeeeeek, eeeeeerrrrrrrr, eeeeeeeeek!

Screamed from the boiling pot.

Sherpa covered her ears and began to cry, her little chin quivering as she tried to remain tough and calm.

"What's wrong, little Sherpa?" Mortimer asked her.

"I don't want to hear dem scream in pain. I heard dat lobsters scream and now I know for myself," she answered in a shaky voice.

"You wanna hear something, Sherpa? I know it'll make you feel better," he said while leaning in closer, she nodded her head yearningly. "It's just expanding air rushing out of the holes in the lobster's shell. They couldn't even scream if they wanted to because they don't have vocal cords. A dead lobster will scream just as loud as a live one because they are whistling through their shells, not screaming, little Sherpa," he said calmly while laying a hand on her head.

She wiped the tears from her cheeks and smiled up at him with glistening eyes. "I don't want to be a bad person, Mort," she said.

"Oh, little Sherpa! Why would you say such a thing?" he asked.

"I just feel different, Mort. I feel like everyding is all wrong here," she responded. Mortimer reached into one of his pockets, pulling out a smooth glossy speckled stone.

"Here, take this. You rub your thumb on it when your worried or anxious. Takes all your worries away," he said to her while showing her the indent on the stone for a thumb digit.

Sherpa began rubbing it, smiling up at him and saying, "Dank you, Mort."

"You know what else, if you don't want people to know, just rub the worry stone while it's tucked away in your pocket. No one will know, and you can hide your nerves," he tipped.

"But what about you? What are you gonna use for yer worries?" she asked with concern.

"No need to worry about me, miss Sherpa," he assured.

Chapter Seventeen

It was the following morning and freezing to the Wintuk family whose bodies were used to constant sunshine. Sanjay and Sierra would soon find out that they were considered wimps compared to the other kids' tolerance for cold weather at school. The two of them sat down with their parents and baby sister for breakfast that morning before walking off to school. Mom and dad were staring at their weapon of choice for daily news, while Sherpa stared at her book of the week—a *Curious George* book this time. She glanced up from her book at Sanjay and Sierra as they sat down, staring up at them without moving her head, eyes just peering over her glasses like a disappointed parent. Jovie and Jerry shifted eyes at one another, smiling at her pretend parent role-playing phase.

After Sherpa made a disgruntled face at her siblings for their clumsy entrance, she stared at the plastic honey bear in front of her.

"Sherpa, what are you doing?" Sierra asked while she examined her sister's gaze at the cute condiment.

"Staring at da honey bear," she responded cooly.

"Why?" Sanjay asked.

"It's lookin' at me funny," Sherpa responded while pointing an interrogating fork in its direction.

"I got a question for ya! Why you so sweet?" she said to the honey bear as if she were a detective.

The whole rest of the family began to laugh hysterically at this, Jerry yelling now, "Where does she come up with this stuff!"

Sierra and Sanjay began their fifteen or so minute walk to school—depending on how much they were dragging their feet that day. As they approached the stairs leading up to the front, they saw Mrs. Minx. Mrs. Minx was drop-dead gorgeous, she basically looked like the real-life version of Jessica Rabbit, she had it all. It'd be safe to assume Sanjay had a type—redheads. She had perfect curves, a plump ass, and a bosom that rose and fell as she breathed. She was breathtaking, especially to puberty inhibited teens who were still experiencing horny triggers on a daily basis.

"Can I give you a piece of advice?" Sierra asked her brother while she noticed his awe towards Mrs. Minx. He nodded while still staring, "Do us both a favor and try your hardest not to call her Mrs. Tits," she said. He snapped out of his daydream and gave her a glare paired with a snarl. Sierra laughed it off and said, "Well, it's the truth, buddy. Why don't you try looking at the two dots in her eyes instead." Sanjay was dumbfounded by his sister's comment as she turned to walk away.

———

Back at home, Jerry, Jovie, and Sherpa were all finishing their breakfast and last slurps of coffee; well for Sherpa, milk.

"Sluuuuuurrrrp, ahhhhh," Jovie and Sherpa did in sync.

"What do ya say we go to the lighthouse and look through the telescope?" Jovie said.

"No!" Sherpa yelled back, reaching into her pocket to use her worry stone. Deep down Jovie and Jerry both knew why she had a phobia of staircases—well, only spiral ones that is. Innocent little vulnerable Sherpa's mind still believed that day in the redwoods with the spiral staircase was just a horrible nightmare. Though, Jovie and Jerry didn't want this 'nightmare' to deter her away from exploration.

"C'mon sweetie, it'll be ok, you think mommy and I would ever do anything to put you in harm?" Jerry asked her.

"Not on purpose," Sherpa responded while looking down at her Winnie the Pooh socks, wiggling her cozied toes while she still rubbed the stone in her pocket.

Jerry and Jovie turned and both looked at each other, this time the stare said, *She's gonna be smarter than the other two*. They could both feel Sherpa staring at them as they peered over to her lowering her glasses at them, like a teacher who just caught two students whispering.

"Is der a problem?" she inquired while they looked back at each other again. Now with stares that said, *Did she learn that from you? No, you?*

The three of them walked out the front door towards the lighthouse, Sherpa whimpering the whole way.

"Sherpa, look!" Jovie exclaimed while pointing out towards the sea.

"Is dat Mort?" Sherpa questioned.

"Yes! Wow, you must have really good eyes!" Jerry said enthusiastically.

Sherpa gave him a funny look, pushing up her glasses with one finger, "Mort is the only person in dis place dat wears a neon orange beanie."

I suppose she's right, Jerry thought to himself as he began to remember that Sherpa doesn't respond well to exaggerated compliments like most children would. She was too smart for that. She stood there quietly, staring into the sea. Jovie wondered what her daughter was thinking, she could always tell when she was deep in thought, she could almost see the reflection of the wheels turning in her head through her pupils. She learned not to interrupt her daughter's thought process, instead to just wait patiently until Sherpa's puzzle pieced thoughts fell into place. Sherpa's eyes widened now as Jovie could see she must just had an epiphany.

"I will only go if I'm carried da whole time," she bargained.

"Deal," Jerry quickly responded, kneeling down for her to jump on his back. The three of them went up the concrete staircase, exiting once at the top to the outdoor area overlooking the sea. You could see Mortimer in the distance, waving up at them. Even though you couldn't see his facial expression, you knew he was smiling while he frantically waved his hand back and forth excitably. The three of them all waved back, Sherpa began clapping her hands now, not only out of enjoyment, but she felt proud that she had finally experienced the lighthouse her siblings spoke of so much.

"See, isn't this great?" Jovie asked her while straightening her glasses that always appeared too large for her tiny chubby face.

"Wanna take a look in the telescope, Sherpa?" Jerry asked. Sherpa nodded her head in agreement and clapped her hands once again. Jerry began to kneel down so that she could stare out.

Sherpa smiled to herself as she peered through the telescope with one eye closed as the other glanced around. She was smiling because she felt like a pirate, and the thought of her being one made her laugh.

"Aaaaaargh!" she said while staring up at her mom with one eye closed still.

"I didn't know we had a pirate as a daughter?" Jerry joked.

"Aaaaargh!" Sherpa said again as viciously as she could.

"She look like a pirate to you, Jove? Cause' she sure sounds like one," he said aloud.

"She looks more like Popeye, if you ask me," Jovie said while giggling. Jovie and Jerry both laughed with one another after this comparison.

"Who dat?" Sherpa questioned. She wasn't impressed and leaned into the telescope once again. Mumbling pirate noises to herself this time…"Aaaarrrgh…"

She could see Mortimer in his boat, rising up and down over the slick cold appearing waves. The sea looked more gray than blue that day, mimicking the overcast skies above like a vast mirror. Sherpa watched in awe as she could see something black slithering up and out of the water, coiling up like enormous octopus tentacles. It rose high above with individual suction cups the size of car tires, slamming back down with the force of a breaching whale. Sherpa gasped.

"What is it, sweetie?" Jovie asked. Sherpa leaned back from the telescope and glanced out to the sea to examine Mortimer was completely fine and unharmed. She inched in again as she took another look, now the beastly sea creature was rising.

Up…

Up…

Up.

It was *him*. *He* had the body of a deep black massive squid, but where the squid's head should have been was his torso rising up with that familiar bat-looking face filled with malicious intent.

"Why are you looking all the way up there?" Jovie asked as she waved her hand in front of the sight of view. Jerry stood back up with Sherpa still hugging his back like a spider monkey.

He noticed where the telescope had been aimed and put in his two cents as well, asking "Yea, Sherpa, what's up there?" Sherpa began to cry and sob now, fogging up her glasses with tearful condensation.

"I—I—I saw *him*," she whispered. "Dis whole time, I thought he was just from a dweam, but I saw *him*!" she cried out in frustration and fear as her crying shoulders bounced up and down.

"Hunny, we didn't see anything," Jerry pointed out calmly.

"Let's go back down," Jovie gestured. The three of them sat on the grass once they exited the lighthouse, trying to bask in the one patch of sunlight that was left. Jovie and Jerry both comforted their baby girl as she cried, hugging and kissing her even though she was snotting all over the place like a piglet. Mortimer could be seen approaching them, with his usual bucket of morsels.

Sherpa ran over to him yelling, "Mort!" He set the bucket down, opening up his arms wide for her to run into, she jumped into his arms as they embraced.

"What's the matter, Sherpa?" he asked while moving her stringy hair from her eyes.

"I got scared and thought a sea monster got you," she said with big watering eyes.

"Oh, Sherpa! You think the Loch Ness got me!" he yelled with an adventurous look as his pupils enlarged.

He set her back down and said, "I got something for you that might make you feel a wee bit better." He began unzipping one of his cargo pockets on his pants, "Aha! Here you go, little Sherpa." He handed her a bouquet of lily of the valley flowers. "Was in my fishing net when I pulled it up out of the water. I thought to myself, you know who would like these? Little Sherpa!" he exclaimed while patting her on the head. "I know they are a bit soggy, but still pretty, right?" he said.

<h1 style="text-align:center">Chapter Eighteen</h1>

Sherpa stomped back over to her parents and threw the soggy white flowers down, saying, "Now I know I wasn't dweaming!" She rubbed the tears from her cheeks and then immediately started pinching her arm for verification. She let out a "Humph!", as she marched towards the house. She could hear her parents apologizing to Mortimer quickly as they politely excused themselves to go comfort their daughter. Once inside the house, they cradled Sherpa, Jovie began sobbing now too out of fear for her family. All of the fear she was experiencing before back in Oyster Shoals, was all regurgitating back up.

"Ok, ok, ok" Jerry kept saying to himself as he paced back and forth across the creaky wooden floors, hands on either side of his head. "I'll be right back, just stay here," he said as he grabbed his coat.

"Jer, where are you going?" Jovie asked.

"Taking Sierra and Sanjay out of school, I'll be right back," he answered.

Sanjay sat in class as Mrs. Minx stood in the front, lecturing the students. Sanjay couldn't tell you what the lecture was about since her voice faded out in his mind as he daydreamed about her body. Watching her ass as she walked back and forth in front of the board, pointing at things and asking questions to the class. Sanjay began to smell rotten eggs, as he reached up and covered his nose with his shirt.

"Hi," was said in a deep voice from the corner of the classroom. Sanjay quickly shot his eyes in the direction of the voice and saw *him* sitting at Mrs. Minx's desk. "I fouuund youuu," *he* tauntingly said to Sanjay as *he* smiled, showing off that devilish toothy grin. *He* stood up from the desk and walked towards Mrs. Minx, now pretending to penetrate her from behind. Sanjay began to shake in his seat as he realized what was going on, not to mention no one else could see *him*.

"Leave her alone," Sanjay mumbled.

"What's that, Sanjay?" Mrs.Minx asked.

"I—I—," was all Sanjay could let escape from his lips.

"Answer the damn broad!" *he* yelled now. *He* pointed at Mrs.Minx's chest, making a button fly off, then another, and another, as *he* laughed the whole time.

"Oh my!" she gasped as she quickly closed her top in confusion.

On the other hand, during this time, Sierra was in the girl's bathroom. She walked out of the stall, approached the sink and washed her hands, analyzing her face in the mirror as she did so. She turned to the side, determining if she was skinny enough or not. Then, grabbing her breasts, trying to determine if those were big enough or not. She wasn't satisfied as she kept pushing them up, then letting them go as they dropped back down, making a defeated face. Then she leaned closer into the mirror, inspecting some acne on her jawline, and pulled out some chapstick to coat her dry lips.

"Puberty is so much fun, isn't it?" a voice questioned from behind. Her heart sank as she turned around to investigate the sarcastic comment. She glanced down the row of closed stalls, and could undeniably see the culprit. One of the stalls had those familiar black obsidian like horns sticking out from the top. Sierra froze, she physically could not move her legs as she saw the horns slowly turn, facing her direction now.

The door unlocked as *he* came out, clapping *his* claws now and saying flamboyantly, "Hormones are raging, emotions are stacking up! Oh, but those hormones, Sierra! Those hormones are getting all out of whack!" *He* leaned into the mirror now, touching *his* face with a long dagger-shaped nail, "Shoot, I really need to do something about my skin," turning to look at her. Sierra could feel her legs again, turning and running out the bathroom door.

As she ran out, skidding around a corner, she could see her brother walking through the hallway.

"Sanjay!" she yelled as she ran to him.

"Sierra!" he returned the yell. They embraced one another as they could both feel each other's heartbeat through the others' chest. "You saw *him* too, I'm assuming?" Sanjay asked.

Sierra let out an exhausted, "Yeah."

"Dad is waiting for us in the office, come on, let's go," Sanjay said. Relief fell over both of them as they saw their dad standing there in the office, though they could sense an urgency in his stance. The three of them made their way back home, power walking through the quiet neighborhood.

Jerry could tell they were shaken up, "You guys too?" he questioned. They both nodded their heads at the same time.

"Sherpa too," he said while grabbing their hands on either side of him.

———————

Jovie made her way outside towards the glass greenhouse, it had started sprinkling. She loved being in the greenhouse while it rained, listening to it pitter-patter all around her as she tended to the plants. It didn't rain much back in California, so this was something she was particularly excited about. It reminded her of growing up on the dairy farm her family owned in Madison, Wisconsin. Jovie had fond memories of running through the nearby cornfields with her cousins when it would rain. She thought about this as she walked around inside the greenhouse, inspecting any potential plant care. The rain became harder now, putting a smile across her face.

The smell of rotten eggs filled the air that smelled so fresh before, making Jovie's nose wrinkle. Immediately, she felt uncomfortable, turning her direction towards the greenhouse door. Something large was staring at her from the corner of her eye, she turned to see a black blurry mass on the other side of the glass. Leaning in closer, she wiped the condensation with her shirt sleeve for a clearer look. Nothing. The black mass was no longer there. She had a feeling though it was *him*.

Pop!

"Waaaa!"

Pop, pop, pop!

"Waaaaaa!"

Jovie turned around to find newborn babies dangling from their umbilical cords connecting to the vines. *Just like before*, she thought. Goo and slime covered her once again and was being splattered on the glass walls surrounding her as the egg-like fruits kept expanding and popping open. She looked to her left and what once was a row of potted plants ready to bloom flowers, started bursting open with crying newborns. The flower buds were expanding just like the dangling egg-like fruits, exploding one by one.

She cried out, "Stop it!" Covering her ears, she kneeled down and curled up in the fetal position.

"Mama!" Sherpa yelled out to her. The crying babies stopped.

"Mama, what are you doing?" Sherpa questioned.

"Um, nothing," she answered while getting up casually and brushing her self off. "Nothing," she repeated. She felt like a horrible mother at this moment.

"Ders a lady who keeps knocking at da front door and Boo and I are twying to watch our TV show," Sherpa informed. Jovie exited the greenhouse, scooping Sherpa up with an arm and arranging her onto her hip. Once inside the house, she made her way to the front door to investigate this knocking that Sherpa spoke of. She peeked through the peephole to see a woman standing there with dirty blonde hair, she appeared to be in her forties.

Jovie cracked open the front door, poking her head out, "Can I help you with something?" she asked.

"I must speak to you, may I come inside? Please?" the woman responded.

———————

As they approached the house, a car was seen in the driveway that Jerry didn't recognize—a Subaru

Outback. He couldn't help but scoff at this observation, walking faster now towards the front door. A woman was sitting at the kitchen table with Jovie.

"Jer, this is Carey Bass, Carey, this is my husband, Jerry, and son and daughter, Sanjay and Sierra," Jovie pointed out.

"Where's Sherpa?" Jerry bluntly asked.

"She's upstairs taking a nap. She's got to be emotionally exhausted, let her rest," she answered. "Why don't you two go upstairs for now, please," Jovie said to them, motioning Sanjay and Sierra to move along. Jovie directed her attention at Jerry, "Carey is here to help," she said.

"I came here to share my story, my story about *him*," she added calmly with sorrow-filled eyes.

"The same, *him*," Jovie confirmed while staring at Jerry.

"I read Jovie's novel, '*Soul Stalker,*' and well…I knew she had experienced the same thing as me. Even though she claimed it's just a fictional story, I knew it was real. Too many coincidences. Even right down to the lily of the valley bouquets and the staircase in the woods," she pointed out. "When you mentioned Porte, Maine in the story, that's when I knew I had to find you. I want to help you before it's too late like it was for my baby boy," she pleaded. Jerry and Jovie looked at each other, trying to read one another's eyes, searching for any sort of emotion. Carey studied this and chimed in, "Let me ask you both something. Do you even remember how you got here? How did you guys get to Porte, Maine?" she inquired.

Jovie and Jerry stared at each other again, "Well…we drove," Jerry answered.

"You did? You remember that? Where's your car?" she asked.

You could see confusion consume Jovie's face, "Where is our car, Jer?" she asked.

"I've been here for twelve years, and I still can't tell you how I got here. The last thing I remember was, I was hiking in some redwoods in Washington with my boy. At first, I think I thought I had driven here…I thought it was my idea to move here—but when I really dug deep into my memories, I realized I didn't drive here, and it wasn't my idea. I think I made myself believe that, or something did, in order to cover up the truth," she explained.

Jovie could feel that painful lump of an emotional bullet lodged in her throat. She held it there, tight in her throat as she thought about it.

"The only reason you guys moved here, is because *he* got into all of your heads. You will realize that people you meet here, are altered versions of people you knew previously," Carey went on.

"What?" Jerry asked in disbelief.

"I'm telling you, it's like the Stepford Wives of Hell here, I can't make this shit up," she continued.

"Is Mortimer like an…altered version of Angus?" Jovie asked herself aloud.

Little did the adults know that Sierra and Sanjay were eavesdropping from the top of the stairs. They both looked at each other at this overheard discovery and whispered, "Mrs. Tits!"

"I just knew something was weird about this place," Sanjay added.

"Me too!" Sierra whispered. They both leaned in with their listening ear perked up.

"Do me a favor, and think of something that happened before you got here, a time between your first encounter with *him* and now, that can't be reversed," Carey asked.

"Lexi being dead," Jerry blurted out.

"She's dead!" Jovie asked, then covering her mouth after realizing she was too loud.

"I saw her dead in Angus's house…I didn't tell you," he added.

"Go online or call her up, you'd be surprised I bet," Carey said.

"I can't believe you didn't tell me she was dead!" Jovie whispered at him.

"I honestly didn't even remember she was until now, Jove!" he said while throwing his hands on his head. "I don't even know whats happening anymore," he murmured.

"Time basically freezes from around the time you meet *him*, at least that's what I've gathered from the last twelve years of being stuck here," Carey responded.

"Well, surely we can leave," Jovie said.

"Trust me, you can't," Carey replied back. Jovie suddenly started remembering a previous time where they tried driving out of the town in a rental car, but it was like some unseen force wouldn't let them leave, making them turn around. Though, Jovie remembered them all convincing one another that they should just turn around, like it was their idea to not leave. Carey could see the realization on her face, "*He*'s good at fogging up the mind."

"Do you know why *he*'s doing this to us?" Jerry questioned.

"I think kids, particularly the younger ones make *him* stronger. Besides that, I think it's just because *he*'s a demon. It's a game to *him,* we're just his pawns in a malicious match," she answered. "By reading your book, I know you had an experience with a staircase in the woods. So did we, and I don't think that's just a coincidence," she continued. "I think the staircases…are like a portal for *him,* and we're stuck in it. Time stops when your stuck here, I haven't aged at all in the last twelve years, ever since I got here. I can't even tell you what day my birthday is, I can't remember anymore."

Chapter Nineteen

Knock, knock.

Jovie answered the front door to find Mortimer standing there, she motioned her arm welcoming him in. Cordial introductions were made as one would expect and Carey started in on the questions again.

"Mr. Mortimer, how long have you been in Porte, Maine?" she asked.

"Hmm…," he thought aloud as he stroked his beard, "since the seventies I'd say."

"Where did you move here from?" Carey continued on like a detective.

"Oregon," he answered.

Jovie was flabbergasted by this, "Mortimer, I thought you said you moved here from Portland? I thought you were always in Maine?" she asked.

"No, I should have clarified, I moved here from Portland, Oregon. Not Portland, Maine," he answered. Jovie sat there and thought about this, a cloud of mysteries swirled around above her head. "Funny thing, sometimes I can't even remember why I moved here. I lived in the most perfect little house near some redwoods," he blurted out.

The room fell silent. Suddenly, Mortimer became visibly upset, crying into his dirty old dry hands. He walked over to his favorite cupboard, or in his eyes—a medicine cabinet, and poured himself a glass of whiskey. Jerry, Jovie, and Carey all stared at one another, not quite sure what just happened or why.

Jerry reached over to him, "Mort?" he asked the old man. Mortimer slammed the glass of whiskey back and poured another one, grabbing a kitchen towel to soak up his tear-filled wrinkles from his face.

"My grandson," was all he could get out before choking up and crying into his palms again. Jerry and Jovie gave each other a mutual stare, this one saying, *I think we're going to learn something new right about now.*

"Bobby was his name. He—he—he committed suicide when he was only eight," he said in a dark melancholy filled voice. "Bobby was under my care, his parents were both out of the picture. Neither one was fit, both druggies. I should have been keeping a closer eye on the boy, but I honestly was so distracted all the time, fixing up old cars in my garage and sucked into my crossword puzzles. You know, a retired old man, just doing retired old man stuff," he said with a guilty tone. The others all tried to comfort him, laying hands on his shoulders simultaneously out of support and genuine concern. "Everything was great before, but after we moved here, that's when Bobby took his own life. Walked up a staircase in Scarlow Forest and jumped from it. Who the fuck puts a staircase in the middle of a goddamn forest!" Mortimer began yelling, irate now.

"*He* does," Carey chimed in. Mortimer slowly looked up at Carey, confusion smeared across his face. The rest of that evening was filled with the adults talking about *him*—and how to stop all of this. They shared experiences and heartfelt emotions with one another, all while Sanjay and Sierra stayed put on the stairs…listening.

"This is all making sense now, pieces are coming together for me, after so many years of being stuck here…after I read your story Jovie, I knew—I just knew that *he*—must start in the redwoods. That's the place, the beginning," Carey said calmly now. "That's the beginning of all of this," she said again.

Sanjay and Sierra both looked at each other at this comment, Sanjay whispered to his sister, "Then what's the end?" Sierra gave her brother a shoulder shrug indicating she didn't know. They could hear Mortimer saying his good-byes as he stumbled into furniture. There was no need to see this visually to know that he was drunk off of too many shots and swigs of—ahem, medicine.

Bang! Boom! Clank!

Could be heard along his pathway to the front door.

They could hear Carey now saying her good-byes, as Jerry insisted on walking Mortimer back home. The two siblings knew this was their queue to get the hell out of there before silence fell in the house. Once the guests were out, they knew mom and dad could hear everything, especially tiny footsteps on the second floor. They quickly separated into their bedrooms, closing the bedroom doors as quietly and softly as possible, both making grimacing faces as they did so.

Jerry and Mortimer began walking out into the cold stinging night, as the breeze swept into Jerry's tear ducts, making his eyes water and blur.

"You don't have to do this!" Mortimer slurred.

Come on old man, Jerry thought to himself as he squeezed Mortimer's arm tighter, picking up the pace more now.

"Slow down!" Mortimer yelled sloppily.

"It's freezing Mort, I walk fast when I'm cold, like most people," Jerry pointed out.

"You damn Californians! Don't know shit!" he mumbled as he drooled, wiping his slobber with his shirt sleeve.

"Come on, let's go, Mort," Jerry pressured. They finally made it to his house within a quick fifteen minutes, though it felt like forty-five to Jerry. This was Jerry's first time stepping foot inside Mortimer's house, or even on his property for that matter. He always knew where the old man lived but kept his distance. His house wasn't messy or dirty, but a little cluttered, it felt somewhat overcrowded but cozy at the same time. There were mason jars everywhere, no light switches, and no electricity for that matter. Mortimer lit a few oil lamps as they walked in, now walking to all the windows to close any open curtains.

Meow.

Jerry jumped, obviously spooked. He wasn't expecting that. Mortimer walked over to the large Maine Coon, scratching its head and kissing its face.

"Whose my handsome boy? Are you my handsome boy? Wow, look at your mane, you look like a little lion," Mortimer was saying lovingly to the cat.

I've never seen this man show as much love to anything or anyone until now. Ugh, is he doing baby voices now? Jerry thought to himself.

"Didn't know you had a cat," he commented.

"Yes, he's my handsome boy," Mortimer responded.

"What's his name?" Jerry asked.

"Handsome boy, but you can call him Handsome for short," he replied.

"Would you like to pet him?" Mortimer asked.

"Er—no, I'm actually allergic to cats," Jerry responded.

"Ugh, of course, you are—you would be," Mortimer said while giving an eye roll.

What the fuck was that? Maybe it's the alcohol talking, Jerry thought, brushing the insult off.

"Are you living in the pioneer days or what?" Jerry asked.

"Ha! You laugh now, but trust me, I'm living for survival. Survival of the fittest, Jerry," Mortimer responded.

"You don't have to live like this, you know," Jerry added.

"You know how ignorant you sound right now, Jerry? I choose to live like this. If anything ever happened—I know I could fend for myself. I could support myself. What could you do? What would you do without your grocery stores, electronics, and technology, huh? You would wither away and die. That's what you would do. Humans are spoiled these days, everything is too easy. One of these days the human race will be tested," Mortimer responded.

"You sound like a worrywart to me," Jerry said.

"You sound like an idiot to me. Anything could happen, the world is a crazy place full of crazy people—"

"—Yeah, like you"

"All I'm saying is, nothing lasts forever. People don't realize how much us humans, as a species, we take advantage of our developments and advancements. Too much of a good thing could be bad. Instant gratification is a sign of weakness, Jerry," Mortimer adds.

"Ok, old man, you've had enough to drink. You should rest and take it easy," Jerry said while walking out the door.

After babysitting duties for the drunk were completed, Jerry made his frigid journey back home. *Maybe the old man has a good point, anything could happen. I mean, I didn't think my family and I would be getting harassed by a demon,* he thought to himself. "Goddammit," he whispered out of frustration that now he could feel his pinky toes becoming numb. "Almost there," he reassured himself, and his pinky toes…in a weird way. As he approached home, he could see an odd shadow being cast from the lighthouse beacon onto the ocean. It was an enormous shadow illuminated onto the calm sea, it was breathtaking at first, however, Jerry soon realized it was the shadow of a head with two devilish horns. His eyes gazed up towards the top of the lighthouse to see *him* standing there, waving.

"Oh come on, Jerry!" *he* yelled, "at least pretend like your excited to see me!" Jerry stood there frozen, but not from being cold, from the fear intensity level rising within his body. "I know, I know…people would respond much better if my shadow cast a Batman symbol or something like that, but I just can't hide these horns, Jerry," *he* said condescendingly as he reached up to touch them. "I'm very insecure about them," *he* continued, obviously just being sarcastic now.

"Oh! It's your lucky day, Jerry," he said while looking down at his wrist, that displayed no watch. "Someone wants to make a deal with the devil, we'll catch up later though, I promise. No hard feelings," he said sardonically again as he breathed arrogance. He was gone and the beacon light shone a normal glow over the sea again, radiating off the dark blue curtain of ripples.

———————

Sanjay wiggled and tossed back and forth throughout the night as he started dreaming. *He* was visiting Sanjay's imagination that night. The dream had started out quite pleasant, as he and his family, including Mortimer, sat around the dinner table eating the catch of the day, Sanjay's favorite— oysters. Sanjay was throwing them back and slurping them up like his life depended on it, as his sister's gagged and mumbled "snot bullets" under their breaths.

"They're delicious, aren't they Sanjay?" Mortimer implied.

"Mhmm!" Sanjay exclaimed as he kept sucking them down. He noticed Mortimer wouldn't stop staring at him, then *his* eyes began to change color, the whites of *his* eyes filling up with blood now as *his* irises became a solid black. Two horns were slowing growing from *his* head as *his* face started molding and twisting into *him*. Sanjay froze as he watched the transformation take place in front of his eyes, still holding an oyster in one hand. He could feel it move as he looked down and the fleshy oyster began to extend and slither out like a tongue, wrapping around his arm.

Up…

Up..

Up.

He screamed as the bowl of oysters all started doing this, quickly extending their slimy flesh out like tentacles, wrapping around Sanjay.

His family giggled at his expense, as *he* laughed and yelled, "The world is your oyster, Sanjay!"

Sanjay shot straight up in bed, panting and breathing heavily like he had just finished a marathon. He was covered in sweat, uncomfortable now as the cool air that seeped in through his closed, but somewhat uneven window hit his wet skin. He pulled the covers tighter around him, cocooning himself in its comfort, going under now and tucking the covers under his head. "It was just a dream, it was just a dream…" he kept repeating to himself as his breathing began to stabilize again.

Chapter Twenty

"I can't believe I'm actually considering this," Mortimer said to himself as he sat on his living room couch. His mind was racing with ideas, both irrational and logical, not sure which way to lean. His hand shook as he took another swig out of a whiskey bottle and held a cigarette in the other. *He* sat in the couch chair across from Mortimer, leaning from side to side constantly and crossing and re-crossing his legs, trying to get comfortable.

"Well, look—I'm only giving you one chance to make a deal with me old man," *he* said impatiently.

"Fine, I'll do it. I'll do it for Bobby," Mortimer whispered, beginning to cry again.

"That a boy!" *he* said while slapping Mortimer's back, *his* claw getting stuck midway as *he* tried to unhook it like a cat.

The following morning, Mortimer made a plan, a plan that would hold up his end of the demon's bargain. He needed to get Sherpa to walk up those stairs and jump willingly for the deal to work, for Bobby to come back. *The demon even said himself it would be harder this time around since she's already done it once—well, halfway.* All *he* kept saying was that some maggot fool jumped instead of Sherpa, ruining it all. Not only that, but it was a given that Sherpa was a sharp kid. Though, Mortimer also knew that Sherpa was an unselfish one too, which he could use to his advantage.

Mortimer walked up to the Wintuk's front door and knocked, hearing a voice yell, "Come in!" Jerry, Jovie, and Carey sat there at the kitchen table, all cupping coffees in their hands.

Why were they all cupping their mugs with two hands clasped around it? Mortimer thought to himself. *What is this? The Depression?* He continued conversing in his head. The three of them stared at him, waiting for some sort of response or movement.

"Look, I uh, er, have been thinking…I've been thinking I want to go back to Scarlow Forest, where Bobby…you know," he said as sorrowful as possible.

"That may be dangerous," Carey pointed out.

"I know, I know, but I think I have a plan to help us, but we all need to be there, we all need to go," he continued on.

"Even the kids?" Jovie questioned.

Mortimer walked over to her and Jerry, putting a hand on either shoulder, "I love you both very much. Trust me on this one. Have I ever let you down?" he assured.

"Yea when I had to walk you home in the freezing night less than twenty-four hours ago," Jerry blurted.

"You know, it might help us to find some answers," Carey now switching gears, thinking about her own child that had jumped from the same staircase in Scarlow Forest.

"So, let me get this straight, you both now think it's a good idea to explore this area, with our kids, where your kids—grandson, committed suicide? I don't think so," Jovie responded.

"Jovie, just hear me out, you've told me what you and your family—the kids, what they've all experienced and endured. If we all go back, maybe we will find answers," Carey explained.

"No! Absolutely not!" Jovie said now in her best mama bear voice.

"Jove, if we sit here, not doing anything, that's just as bad. We're trapped, Jove," Jerry said.

"I don't want the babies to be trapped," she murmured now, sobbing uncontrollable and leaning into her husband's chest.

"I know, I know," he said while stroking her hair.

That evening Jerry and Jovie sat their three rascals down to prepare them—sort of.

"Take these," Jovie said as she passed the three of them each a can of pepper spray.

"Jove, really?" Jerry said while looking at her in disbelief.

"Better than nothing, Jer" she replied. "Alright, so this is how you lock it and unlock it," she explained to them while giving a visual presentation.

"Why does Sanjay get the blue one and Sherpa and I have to have the pink?" Sierra asked.

"Um, well, I guess I just assumed" she said while shrugging her shoulders.

"You ass-ass-assumed wong," Sherpa stuttered back. Jovie and Jerry looked at each other, giggling a little at this sentence consuming both the words 'ass' and 'wong.'

"How old are we, Jer?" she asked as they both continued to laugh, shaking their heads at how immature they both felt.

"Fifty and fifty-three," Sherpa announced without hesitation.

Sanjay and Sierra both glanced at their sister, "I didn't even know that," Sanjay said.

"Me neither," Sierra chimed in.

"You guys, we're just going for a hike with Mortimer and our new friend Carey, there's no need to be scared. I think the pepper spray may be overkill…" Jerry said while glancing over at Jovie.

"Better safe than sorry, bucko," she said while raising her eyebrows at him.

"Ha! Yea, speaking of bucko, I'd hate to end up like that buck you shot…" Jerry responded cooly.

"That wasn't even a buck, it was an animabus damnatis, remember?" Sanjay said.

"What?" Sherpa asked.

"You guys, stop, just focus, listen to what I'm telling you, and how to use this stuff just in case—please," Jovie implied.

"Why does the side of this pepper spray say *'Damsel in Distress'*?" Sanjay questioned.

Jovie slapped the front of her forehead, pronouncing each syllable now, "Fo-cus, please Sanjay."

"It's the company name, San-jay," Sierra said, imitating her mom's pronunciation of syllables.

"Dank you, Captain Obvious," Sherpa said while staring up at her older sister. She struggled with that last word, but surprisingly it came out correct.

"Where does she get this stuff from, Jove?" Jerry asked as his face transformed red from holding in laughter.

"Focus!" Jovie yelled now, making the house almost feel like it shook. "This is serious!" she continued to say. They all stared at her like good little students, clasping their hands together, and sitting up straight. "Now pay attention, I want us all to be prepared for our hike into Scarlow Forest tomorrow," she said.

———————

The Wintuks pulled into the parking lot of the hiking area for Scarlow forest. They could see Carey and Mortimer were already there, parked and ready to go, standing outside of their vehicles.

"Why Suburu Outbacks? Why?" Jerry asked as they pulled their rental car in.

"I don't know Jer, just drop the whole Suburu thing, will ya?" she barked back. Her mid-west accent coming out thicker with the more annoyed she became. The family got out of the car and met up with the other two.

"Well, shall we then?" Mortimer said while motioning towards the entrance to the forest.

They hiked through the damp misty forest that smelled of rain and pine with a hint of dirt. It was magnificent, quite different then any hikes or ventures they'd been on the west coast. The air was crisp and felt almost rough on the skin, but didn't bother any of them as you could hear them all taking turns breathing in and out saying, "Ahhh." Breathing in felt like you were sucking up the surrounding fog, and releasing it as you breathed out. The idea of this was fun for Sherpa, though everyone else knew it was just fucking cold.

"I'm having trouble remembering where to turn off the beaten path, Carey," Mortimer admitted.

"You and me both," she confessed as they all continued trucking. He looked around trying to locate any sort of déjà vu or clue that would help guide the way.

There! Mortimer noticed a tiny cluster of lily of the valley flowers, which he kept to himself. "I, uh, I feel like it's somewhere over here," he said in his best play-dumb voice he could sputter while stepping on the white flowers.

Continuing off the beaten path, the group finally approached a spiral staircase in the middle of a circle of pine trees. In the center of the spiral staircase though, was a tall slender pine tree boosting up towards the sky, the staircase wrapping ever so delicately around it. Carey's eyes began to water with a current of emotions as she thought about her son, Jerry reached over and laid a hand on her shoulder.

"You ok?" he asked her. She nodded, indicating for them all to continue on despite her nostalgic uproar of despondency.

The ground began to shake as they all stood there trying to balance their stance as their equilibriums quaked. The earth opened up like a whale shark's mouth, ready to vacuum up any microorganisms. *He* levitated out of the hole, landing on two talon-like feet as it closed behind him.

"Miss me?" *he* asked all of them.

"I knew this was a bad idea," Jovie said aloud to herself.

Mortimer reached over and held Sherpa's hand, leading her towards the spiral staircase. "Mortimer, what are you doing?" Jerry asked as he moved to interfere. *He* swung a claw in the group's direction, making them all freeze, held against their will as they watched in fear. Sherpa began to cry and whimper, trying to pull away from Mortimer.

"C'mon Mort! Get a move on with it. Tell her whatever she needs to hear, remember—willingly," *he* demanded.

Mortimer looked over at Sherpa, a tear rolled down his cheek as he kneeled to her level, "Sherpa, sweetie, you've got to listen to me…" was all that could be heard escaping from his lips.

Sherpa's family all began screaming, yelling to her "No, Sherpa! Don't listen, Sherpa!" Until *he* motioned a claw over towards their direction once again, forcing their mouths shut. Mortimer was still kneeling down, talking to Sherpa, but no one could hear what he was whispering. Sherpa could be seen nodding her head like she understood and agreed as they both turned towards the staircase. The Wintuks could all feel their hearts sink as they watched in horror.

The two of them held hands as they walked up the stairs, while *he* sat there grinning with drool dripping out the corner of *his* mouth, sliding down *his* chin. *His* eyes lit up once they reached the top step. Sherpa looked down below where the hole once was that *he* came out of, her legs began to shake a little as she grasped one hand on the railing and the other still holding Mortimer's hand.

She looked up at him, "Mort? Will it hurt?" she asked.

"No sweetie, it'll be ok, I promise. Won't feel a thing," he assured. Mortimer leaned over and kissed her on the forehead, wiping tears from her soft cheeks. He grabbed her other hand and placed it on the railing, then turned out towards the opening and fell forward to his death.

"No! No! No! The whole thing is messed up again!" *he* screamed as *he* pounded *his* fists into the ground, making beastly grunts and growls. "What the fuck am I supposed to do with this!?" *he* asked himself while motioning over to Mortimer's lifeless body. "I can't do anything with this piece of shit!" *he* growled.

"He not a piece of shit!" Sherpa cried out defensively.

Everyone could feel their bodies again as they darted towards the staircase to Sherpa's aid. They climbed up the stairs as Sherpa was making her way down them, meeting about halfway, embracing one another and crying into shaking shoulders. *He* glared at little Sherpa, that familiar smile spreading across *his* face, nostrils flaring.

"Oh yes, he is Sherpa. Tainted souls like his don't do me any good, I need pure innocent ones like yours to make me stronger. The older humans become, the less innocent they get. The older humans become, the more they learn. The more they learn, the more they realize. Realize what it means to sacrifice," *he* growled.

Soon they noticed it wasn't just their crying shoulders shaking, but the whole staircase started to shake as it corkscrewed down. It was rotating back down into the forest floor, too fast for them to react as the last thing they saw before complete darkness was *him*, pointing a claw at them yelling, "You fucking maggots!"

Chapter Twenty-One

It was oddly dark, that it almost seemed uncomfortably loud. The Wintuks never realized a visual sensory could appear loud until now. Light could be seen finally! They all gazed up as they could see the daylight getting closer and closer to them. They began corkscrewing up out of a different forest floor this time, and it felt warmer, the air dryer then where they were before. As the staircase rose between the trees, Sierra could see that familiar amber sap seeping out from the redwood trunks. The staircase stopped moving as they all sat there, confused and somewhat in shock.

"Why do I feel like we're not in Porte anymore?" Carey asked. Silence filled the air as they all sat there on the steps, trying to absorb it all in.

Music could be heard now, Jovie jumped up, yelling with excitement,"It's-it's—it's The Talking Heads! '*This must be the place*'! Come on, follow me!" she said while leading them down the stairs. She followed the music as the rest of them followed her, the music getting louder and louder until they made it out of the redwoods, facing two cars blaring their speakers. It was the Subaru Outbacks…right where they left them on that day when they came to find Sherpa.

"Jump in!" Jovie yelled.

"Damn Subaru Outbacks," Jerry could be heard mumbling to himself.

Carey went to get in the other vehicle on her own, "Carey?" Jovie asked. "Carey, we can all pile in one, I don't want you to be by yourself," Jovie implied.

"It'll be ok, it's silly for us all to pile in one. You've got kids, I'll be ok," Carey answered. The Wintuks began driving down the road that led out of the redwoods, with Carey following closely behind. Action could be seen flashing between the trees as they realized it was a stampede forming of animabus damnatises.

"They're helping us again!" Sanjay exclaimed. They surrounded both cars, running alongside them, acting as their protectors.

"They're sacrificing themselves…for us," Sierra said.

Cruuuunch!

The sound of a car being destroyed could be heard as Jovie looked up in the rearview mirror to Carey no longer being there. Instead of seeing her following them, it was now a humungous thing resembling a worm…

"What the hell was that!" Jerry yelled. Another fleshy massive worm shot out from the ground, wiggling back and forth like one of those inflatable tube guys you see at sketchy car sale lots. It didn't have eyes, just a large body that flailed about without direction or reason, paired with a mouth that took up basically its whole face—or what would normally be a face. Its mouth was full of sharp pointed serrated teeth and when it would strike, it would rise up and bend over, striking its mouth straight down, hoping to get lucky with a bite to eat. The whole family screamed as they kept dodging the worms attempts to eat them, seeing some animabus damnatises that weren't as fortunate as they were.

The Wintuk family finally made it out of harm's way. As they drove out of the redwoods, Sierra looked out the back window and saw one animabus damnatis waving to her, she raised her hand and waved back. Jerry looked over at Jovie, saying, "By Jove, I think we've got it."

The Wintuks pulled into their driveway, still shaken up about everything that had happened, almost feeling as if the whole experience was a dream. Though, many pinching tests between Sierra and Sherpa proved that the experience was all too real. Jerry dropped his jaw as he saw a big fat Lexi making her way to the mailbox.

"She's…alive. Just like Carey had said," he pointed out, following a gulp. Her beady eyes, appearing too small for her monstrous head, shifted over to them.

"I feel bad about what happened to Carey," Jovie said.

"Me too, but we didn't have any control over what happened. It's a shame though, considering she's part of the reason we made it out alive," Jerry replied. Lexi began waddling towards them like an overweight penguin. *Oh great, let's see how long this takes. Damn pufferfish, too puffy for her own good,* Jerry thought.

After what should have been a ten-second walk, felt like a five-minute walk, Lexi finally made it to their car.

"What the hell happened tae yer motur?" she asked while analyzing all the shattered windows on the car. No one responded quickly enough for her. "It doesn't matter, not any of mah business. Just making wee talk. Let me know if ye see any sign of Angus, he's wandered off again," she said. Jovie and Jerry glanced over at one another, neither sure what to make of this.

"How long has he been missing?" Jerry inquired.

"Since th' wee hours of th' morning," she answered, turning her massive body to walk away.

"Jer, did she not realize we're in one of her dad's cars?" Jovie asked nervously.

"Maybe she didn't even know about the car in the garage? I don't know, but we should all go inside," Jerry advised.

Lexi turned around when she got to the front door, yelling back to Jovie, "Jovie, ah meant tae tell ye!"

"What's that?" Jovie hollered back.

"Happy Mother's Day," Lexi said while giving a smile and a good-bye wave, closing the door behind her. The Wintuks all gazed around at each other, soaking in this piece of information.

"So, I guess its Mother's Day…again," Sanjay pointed out.

"Wanna go inside and open yer Moder's Day gifts, mama?" Sherpa asked.

"I suppose we never had the chance to do that earlier, did we?" Jovie responded, still in shock and stupefaction.

"Let's go inside," Jerry announced.

"Blueberry pancakes?" Sierra proposed.

"Anything but oysters," Sanjay chimed in.

"I thought oysters were your favorite?" Sierra questioned him.

"Not anymore, I'm never getting near those snot bullets again," he confirmed.

"I'm never getting near those redwoods again," Sierra added.

"Me neither," the Wintuks all agreed.

The End

www.ingramcontent.com/pod-product-compliance
Lightning Source LLC
Chambersburg PA
CBHW030748110726